WOLF RANCH: SAVAGE

WOLF RANCH - BOOK 4

RENEE ROSE

VANESSA VALE

Wolf Ranch: Savage

Copyright © 2020 by Bridger Media and Wilrose Dream Ventures LLC

This is a work of fiction. Names, characters, places and incidents are the products of the author's imagination and used fictitiously. Any resemblance to actual persons, living or dead, businesses, companies, events or locales is entirely coincidental.

All rights reserved.

No part of this book may be reproduced in any form or by any electronic or mechanical means, including information storage and retrieval systems, without written permission from both authors, except for the use of brief quotations in a book review.

Cover design: Sarah Hansen / Okay Creations

Cover graphic:

1

LINT

Cooper Valley's lone saloon, Cody's, was packed with a mix of drunken humans and shifters. The twang of country music filled the air along with whoops and hollers from the back corner where people tested their mettle on the mechanical bull. The scent of spilled beer and potent cologne made me wish for wide open spaces. I tossed back another whiskey and watched the blonde nurse weave across the floor for her turn. Tipsy humans weren't usually my thing, but this one was damn cute. Her lush mouth was wide open in a carefree smile, her cowgirl hat askew on her head. She wore a pair of hot pink, cowgirl boots with her short jean skirt that combined to make her the hottest number in the bar. I was jealous of the mechanical bull. If she wanted to go for a ride, she'd get more fun out of my dick. I could promise her that.

Of course, my pack brother, Boyd, would strongly disagree with my desire to sidetrack the nurse from his mate's bachelorette party. The shindig we males crashed.

Boyd and Colton had ridden in a limo with their mates and the other ladies in the group. I'd caught up to them because leaving human females unprotected at a drinking establishment was not a possibility. Boyd and Colton were keeping an eye on their mates, but as council enforcer, it was my secret job to keep everyone safe at all times. Audrey now belonged to the pack, and the way Colton was keeping a protective watch on her sister, growling at any male who came near her, I had a feeling she'd be mated as soon as they found an available horizontal surface.

Lucky bastards.

I accepted another shot and raised my glass to Boyd, who stood a few feet away, protecting his mate. His *pregnant* mate.

Again, lucky bastard. How the cocky fuck found

a human to be his mate, claim her and put a baby in her belly was beyond me. He hadn't been around in years. Returned home for one rodeo event, and he'd been lassoed by a cute Ob/Gyn.

And me? I'd been downing the liquor like it was water, trying to tamp down my wolf's agitation that I hadn't found my own mate yet. I was older than Boyd and Colton and had had plenty of opportunity, not only in Cooper Valley but also as I traveled as an enforcer. I had more reach than most shifter males to find a mate.

Now, looking at the Wolf brothers zeroed in on human females, it occurred to me that maybe I'd been looking in the wrong places.

I hadn't realized a wolf could choose a human for a mate, but clearly they had. It made no sense to me logically, but there was no denying biology. Boyd was certain. Colton looked pretty damn certain too.

I glanced away from the Wolf boys and caught a glimpse of Becky on the bull. Yeah, the hot little number with a jean skirt riding high on her thighs made my dick press painfully against the zipper of my jeans. A human male—damn, actually three human males—lurched toward Becky, the adorable tipsy nurse, as she hopped off the mechanical bull. My wolf growled.

I didn't like males taking advantage of a female who'd been drinking. She might not be my female to specifically protect, but she was here with our group, and I'd be damned if I was going to let any male paw her when she was in this inebriated state. Hell, even if she was stone cold sober.

I downed the two fingers of whiskey and pushed off from the bar, picking my way through the crowd with my gaze glued to the petite blonde.

"—why don't you take a ride on me next?" some asshole said to her.

"Why don't you let me through?" she countered, arching a brow.

Good. She wasn't as drunk as I'd thought. I liked knowing she could take care of herself. Still, I felt obliged to provide back up. It was in my wolf DNA and in my enforcer job description.

"You heard the lady." My deep voice cut through the crowd, and four heads swiveled my way in surprise—the three human men vying for Becky's attention and the lovely nurse's. I didn't get in her space, wanting to give her the room the other guys weren't offering.

She beamed at me from her spot by the rail that enclosed the mechanical bull area. Her blue eyes showed pleasure at seeing me, and I wondered what they'd look like when they showed pleasure from me getting her off. I didn't care if it was on my fingers, on my mouth or on my dick. I'd satisfy her any way she wanted it.

"Thank you, Clint."

It took me a second to recover from surprise that she knew my name, and in that moment, the asshole in question positioned himself between me and my little nurse. Yeah, *my* little nurse because I had my sights set on her. But these assholes were pretty much cockblocking me, which really didn't set well. The fact that they were messing with Becky didn't make me happy either.

"Give the lady some space," I growled. Rob, our pack alpha, my boss and best friend, didn't like us picking fights with humans. Sure, he and the Shifter Council sent me out to deal with rogue shifters or anyone who needed reminding of the rules, but this was different. This was Cody's on a crowded summer night. The temptation to show wolf superior strength was fucking strong, but the chance of truly hurting a human or worse—revealing our nature—would increase. I was careful to keep our ways a secret, but no one fucked with a female, shifter or human.

No way was I backing down.

Especially not when nutsack gave me a shove. I tried not to laugh at his meager strength. I had to be six inches taller and a bag of feed heavier. He did have balls though. I had to give him that. Still—

I wrapped a fist in his shirt and used it to pick him up and shake him. "Get lost, asshole. The lady asked you to let her through."

He threw a punch. I couldn't miss the windup, and I was tempted to dodge it. To throw one back. But the thought of pissing off my alpha ran through my head, so I held still and took it—right in the nose.

Meh. He'd broken it. Whatever. It hurt a little, but I'd heal in a few hours. No biggie.

The worse blow was to my ego, which really wanted me to pound the fuck out of said asshole right here in the bar. But what I wanted to do to him would put him in the hospital, and that was a big no.

Fucking humans.

I sighed and settled for my fingers around his throat. My hands were big and strong. I could squeeze and lift him off his feet at the same time. Blood ran down my face, but the dude was turning purple, gasping and kicking out to reach the floor. I waited a couple beats until Becky closed the distance between us, plucked my sleeve with a sweet little, "Clint." Only then did I drop the guy.

Wolf Ranch: Savage

I let him fall and immediately ignored him, turning all my attention to the little blonde. "You okay, sugar? Come here."

I didn't plan on doing anything dramatic, but one minute she stood before me, her head tilted back so her blue eyes met mine, looking adorable in her pink boots and mini skirt, the next she was up in my arms in a honeymoon carry.

"Clint!" she shouted, laughing.

I pushed through the crowd toward the bathrooms because I was going to have to clean up. I didn't give a shit about blood. Being a nurse, I doubted she did either, but still. On the right were the doors to the restrooms, to the left a storage room. I chose the left where we wouldn't be interrupted.

My sudden flare for the dramatic continued because I didn't feel like dropping her after I opened the door and carried her right inside. Only when I'd found the switch to illuminate the shelf-lined walls did I tip her back onto her feet. I locked the door—not because I was planning on doing anything with her. I just didn't want to be bothered. Yeah, that was all. It wasn't that I wanted uninterrupted alone time with the little nurse.

"Wow, are you all right? That guy was a total

jerk." Her breathless voice wound around my trunk like honey and silk. She looked up at me with the prettiest wide blue eyes I'd ever seen. "We should probably get you to the hospital to have that set."

I smirked at her because her concern was damn cute. The bleeding had already stopped, so I went over to the utility sink, pushed a mop handle out of the way and quickly washed. Tugging a few paper towels from the dispenser, I dried my face. There was some blood on my snap shirt, but that wasn't going anywhere until I got it in the washer. I would take it off though, if she wanted. Fuck, yeah, I would.

I leaned down to put my face close to hers. "You can set it for me, sugar, and we can skip the doctors. Hell, we can play *doctor* if you want."

I grinned at her blush, which I couldn't miss even with the single light bulb lighting the room.

"Oh, well, I don't know—" she said, but still reached up to line her thumbs along the bone of my nose. One quick move, and she snapped it back in place. She didn't flinch, didn't even blink at the task.

I wiggled my nose like a rabbit. "I knew you could do it for me."

"Are you okay?" Her hands slid to my chest. The touch set off something strange inside me. Sure, it made my dick hard, but it was more. A connection.

It must've had something to do with the whiskey. Shifters sobered pretty damned fast, but still. I didn't usually react so... *viscerally* to human women. "That was very gentlemanly of you to step in."

I suddenly wished getting punched in the nose hadn't fucked with my sense of smell because my wolf was itching to get a noseful of her. I'd bet she smelled sweet.

Sweet as candy.

Every-fucking-where.

"I'm fine, sugar." My hands found her waist of their own accord. I shouldn't touch her. Not when she'd been drinking.

I'd been drinking, too.

Plus, she was best friends with my pack brother's mate.

But her waist felt perfect under my palms. She had meat on her bones, and I itched to feel every inch of those soft, lush curves. Her blue gaze had locked onto mine, and she was breathing softly and quickly, little pants that made me want to shove her up against the wall to make them heavier. "You?"

"I'm fine," she said quickly, eyes dilated. "I'm better than fine." She licked her lips. "In fact, I'm kinda turned on by you right now."

Hell, yes. A woman who knew what she wanted

and wasn't afraid to voice her needs. My dick went hard at her honesty.

"That was pretty badass the way you choked that guy with just one hand." She cocked her head toward the closed door. Thankfully, the thick wood muffled the noise and music from the bar.

I almost groaned. My dick had gone rock hard, and she'd stepped so close to me I could feel her body heat, her soft curves just centimeters away. She was a petite, tempting handful.

"Sugar, you're pushing my self-control here." Despite my words, I pulled her soft body up against mine. "No matter how much I want to take things further, both of us have been drinking, so I think I'd better get you home before we get ourselves into trouble."

She smiled up at me, her lids at half-mast. "Trouble, hmm?" she purred. "What if trouble is what I'm looking for?"

This time I was pretty sure my groan escaped. Holy. *Fuck.*

I'd been propositioned before. Becky, though, had my dick leaking pre-cum from just talk. She was fully clothed, and we hadn't even kissed.

"I'm not that drunk." She pressed those pert

breasts against my ribs. "I've been drinking water the past hour."

I took a deep breath, but... nothing. Damn, I had never wanted to smell a female so much in my life. Why'd that asshole have to punch me in the goddamn nose? I'd be able to scent her pussy, know if she was wet just by one inhale. I'd have to find out another way... my fingers itching for the task.

My brain scrambled—something that never happened to me with females—especially not human ones. Hell, my dick took over. Next thing I knew, I used my shifter strength to pick her up and set her down on a table I assumed was used for... hell if I knew or cared. I was just thankful for its existence as I stepped up between her parted thighs. Her jean skirt rode up, and I couldn't miss the hint of hot pink panties... and a wet spot.

Yeah, she was wet for me. I licked my lips, eager to get a taste.

She let out a chuckle of breathy excitement and hooked a hand behind my head to bring my face down to hers. That was the *yes* my wolf and I needed.

She wasn't drunk. She'd said as much, and her behavior was that of a hot, horny woman—not a drunk. I wasn't taking advantage in a storage room.

That would be extraordinarily ungentlemanly. Hell, she just might be taking advantage of me. And that was sure as hell fine with me.

I was unprepared for the sweetness of the kiss. The intensity. Her lips were soft and tasted faintly of strawberries and vodka. Her impetuous tongue swept between my lips, and that was my undoing although I'd been barely holding on before now.

Suddenly, I couldn't hold back at all. I must've had more alcohol than I should have. Or maybe it had been the contemplation of wishing I could have my own mate, but suddenly my focus narrowed to nothing but this moment. This sweet little human before me, offering her mouth up for the taking.

And take it I did.

I fucking *owned* it. And her.

I kissed the hell out of the little nurse until she writhed against me, her ankles hooked behind my back, pulling me against her sweetest spot.

"Clint," she whimpered against my lips, her voice thready with need.

"Yeah, sugar?" I held her jaw, ready to angle my lips back over hers as soon as she finished her piece. I still couldn't smell a thing, which drove me fucking nuts. I just knew she'd smell delicious. Edible, even.

Her eyes dropped to the bulge in my jeans. The

bulge pressed up against her pink satin panties. "Show me what you're packing in there," she murmured, her voice husky.

I shouldn't. I wasn't going to, but my dick was leading the charge.

Her deft fingers popped the button and undid the zipper before I'd even decided how to tell her we shouldn't.

"Aw, sugar, drinking and—*oh*." I choked on the last syllable when she grasped the base of my dick in her tight fist and gave it a tug. Those tiny fingers gripped me tight.

"Do you have a condom, cowboy?" Her smile was knowing and sure, her touch intent. She had plans for my dick.

A shudder of pleasure ran through me. I lengthened in her hand as she jerked me off. Pre-cum dripped down over her fingers.

My brain could barely process for the pleasure, the synapses slow and sparking, but I eventually reached in my back pocket and produced a condom. "Yes, ma'am."

She took it from me and ripped it open with her teeth then rolled the rubber on. I didn't even know if she finished getting it in place because a storm of desire flushed through me, volcanic in nature. I wanted in her. *Now.* I wanted to feel the tight, hot heat of her pussy around me. I wanted to feel the ripples of her pleasure as I fucked her over the edge.

"Come here," I rasped, picking her up so she straddled my waist. Gripping the full swell of each ass cheek, I spun her around until her back was against the wall.

"Oh God, yes." She clung to my shoulders, holding herself up as I shoved her panties to the side and sunk into her heat.

Yes. *Yes.*

A growl filled the storeroom. The thump of music from Cody's dance floor faded. My vision narrowed to myopic level. Nothing mattered except pounding into this sweet, willing human I had nailed to the wall with my dick.

Especially when she started making little noises of agreement. *Uhn. Uhn. Clint.*

Oh, damn. She felt so good. So perfect. So right.

Why hadn't I let off some steam with humans more often? It was definitely worth it. I buried my cock in her sweet heat up to the hilt, eased back, shoved in deep again. I watched her closely, ensuring I was giving it to her how she needed it. I didn't let myself pound as hard as I wanted to for fear I'd hurt her. It didn't matter. Fucking her still felt like heaven. Every time I filled her, I lost a little more control until I was pushing fast and hard, holding my hips close to hers, so I wouldn't slam her against the wall.

Her nails dug into my shoulders, her legs wrapped tight behind my back, the heels of those cowboy boots digging into my ass. She kept making those sounds that drove me fucking crazy.

Holy shit, it had never been this good. This wild, as if I were almost... *savage* for her.

"I'm gonna come, sugar. Are you close?" No way was I leaving her behind.

"*Now*, cowboy," she commanded, like she'd been waiting to say it.

I sped up, jackhammering in and out, while her cries filled my ears. I came with a snarl—the kind of sound I should never let a human hear, but it didn't matter because I was banging the thoughts right out of her head. Her cries matched mine, and I had no doubt anyone in the hall would know what was going on in here. Her tight pussy squeezed my dick like a glove, pulsing and milking it for its cum. And there was a lot of it to fill the condom. I gave her all I had and didn't let up until my balls were fucking empty.

"Oh fates, that was good," I managed to say as my

vision began to clear. I could barely catch my breath as I set her back on her feet.

The little human smiled up at me. Her cheeks were flushed, her eyes all hazy, and my dick started to harden all over again knowing I'd made her look that way. "It sure was."

I eased out, tossed the condom into the trash then tucked myself away and pulled up my pants as she fixed her panties and slid her skirt back down. I'd barely seen any of her, and I wanted another round, but the next time I'd have her naked. She adjusted her top, smoothed her hair down. She might look put back together, but anyone out there would know she'd just been well satisfied.

That made me feel like a million, very cocky, bucks. I wanted to give her that glow again. And again, which had me suddenly remembered why I didn't make a habit of randomly screwing humans.

They had feelings. I couldn't exactly enter a relationship with one when I was holding out for my true mate. No matter how hot a fuck that had been, she wasn't my mate. And I may never have one.

Shit.

I sure as hell hoped Becky didn't get hurt by this.

"You need a ride home?" I asked. "A bottle of water?"

Things suddenly got awkward.

"No." Becky breezed past me and unlocked the door. "I came in the limo, remember?" She glanced over her shoulder and offered me a smile. *She* was reassuring *me*. "Don't get weird about this, okay? We hooked up. We both enjoyed it. End of story."

"Right." I caught up and dropped a hand to her hip to escort her out. "I definitely enjoyed it." The top of my head had pretty much blown off. I opened the door, the sounds of reality crashing around us again.

I enjoyed it way more than I should have. My dick wanted more of that hot pussy, that was for damn sure. Which meant I definitely needed to steer clear of Becky and the temptation she presented. Because my mom raised me better than to toy with the emotions of random females, even if she sure seemed fine with a hot quickie.

2

Clint

Four months later

I sat on the edge of the motel bed to clean my gun and place the silver bullets in the chamber. There weren't many Shifter Council enforcers, and we varied as much as the geography of the packs we were from. There were some enforcers who killed in shifter form. I preferred remaining in human form, the silver bullet from a gun my method of pack justice. I had no idea why—it just felt more civilized.

That didn't mean I hadn't killed with my bare hands. Or teeth.

I had.

But I hoped today I'd be able to use the bullet and keep justice as swift and painless as possible.

I holstered the gun under my arm and pulled a down jacket over my t-shirt to cover it. The moment I stepped outside the wind howled in my ears. Wyoming was fucking windy in November. Hell, Wyoming was fucking windy all the time, in my experience. November might still technically be fall, but it was cold as fuck and would stay that way until at least March.

This wasn't my favorite place to be. I'd been tracking Jarod Jameson, the rogue shifter who was the infamous convenience store killer, across the state for twelve days now.

Unfortunately, I failed to stop him before he'd struck again last night in Gillette. Another convenience store worker had had his throat ripped out. The register had been emptied. The FBI were involved because the spree had crossed state lines, and I needed to put a lid on this thing ASAP.

The agency didn't know shit about shifters, and Jameson needed to be punished by shifter means. To be put down, so he wasn't a threat to the shifter way. To humans.

Late last night, I'd slipped into the scene of the crime in wolf form to scent the place. I pushed past the bleach cleaner used on the floor and the fatty aroma of rotating hot dogs and picked up his scent. I knew it now and would know him when I found him. I didn't need video surveillance or mug shots to identify the guy.

He was a wolf shifter, like me. Fucker. I hated when our species screwed things up in the shifter world. But it made him easier to find and execute. A wolf knew a wolf.

As an enforcer, I knew how to hunt a rogue one.

I'd seen no paw prints in the snow around the building, so I believed he traveled by car. I already knew from the security footage released to the public that he attacked in human form. He must partially shift to maul the workers. No human ripped out another's throat.

Whatever the story, he had to be put down.

Today.

Before he hurt any more humans and exposed our kind to their law enforcement.

My theory was that he was into drugs. That's why the wild, haphazard robberies and random killings, all at convenience stores. Whatever cocktail of narcotics he'd taken had made him crazed. Savage enough to kill innocent people trying hard to make a living.

Whatever his reasoning, it didn't matter. The council had sent me to end him. We didn't allow rogue shifters or human killing.

He might still be alive, but his life was forfeit.

I entered a diner and immediately caught the fucker's scent. Luck was with me. Trouble was, he'd scent me, too. Know a shifter was close. After him. Getting away with a number of killings and staying off the radar of the FBI meant he wasn't just rogue, he was smart.

I turned around and left. It was better to catch him outside and have the element of surprise on my hands. A bunch of diners as witnesses wouldn't be good, either.

In the Wolf pack, only Rob knew I was an enforcer. Sure, the others knew of the role within the pack system, but our identities were secret. While everyone wanted to ensure pack safety and security, no one wanted to know they had an executioner in their pack.

Boyd and Colton had no idea. Neither did my brother, Rand, my parents or anyone else. To them, I worked the ranch. Handled the horses. Was our pack's chosen delegate to the council. A simple cowboy living a simple rural life.

As fucking if.

I walked through the dirt parking lot until I caught the faint scent again around an old Honda Civic. Great, now I had his car. I went back to my truck, parked facing the lot and diner but near the street and climbed in to wait.

Twenty minutes later, a guy moved toward the door, setting a toothpick between his teeth. Just because I'd scented him didn't mean I didn't have his photo. I did my job and did it well. Skipping something like being able to identify the rogue shifter by more than scent was plain stupid. My mind drifted back to that night months ago when I'd fucked the hot little number, Becky, in the storage room. I thought of that often, especially with my dick in hand. I hadn't been able to scent her then, and that had been a fucking shame. I could only imagine what it would have been like if I'd had that sense at the time.

As the guy stopped in the middle of the parking lot to adjust his pants, I put a silencer on the pistol. The place was remote enough that if I could haul him around back, I could be done with this damn assignment.

I jogged toward the guy, his pasty face smudged with bacon grease.

"Jarod Jameson?" I asked, even as I got a whiff of him. I prodded him in the ribs with the muzzle of the gun through my coat pocket.

He started to snarl but then must've caught my shifter scent because he stiffened, and the metallic smell of fear issued from his body.

Be afraid, fucker.

I lifted my chin. "Walk around back."

His movements were jerky as he obeyed, stepping around behind the diner. I prodded him to keep moving until we were all the way behind the dumpster. Glancing around, I confirmed we were alone.

"Jarod Jameson, you have violated shifter law, and the shifter council has deemed your life forfeited," I recited.

Even though I held a gun to his back, he whirled and slashed me with a dagger, far faster than should have been possible, even for a shifter.

Holy fuck. I lurched back, but not before the tip skimmed across my ribs, cutting through my jacket, shirt and flesh. It shouldn't have hurt all that much because it was a shallow graze across my ribs, but the gash immediately began to sizzle and pop, like the tip had been poisoned. Probably with silver.

Shit. It wasn't going to kill me, but it was going to hurt like fuck. And slow me down. My body had to work hard to fight the poison, and that meant less healing properties and less focus.

I ignored the searing pain, trying to keep my vision clear.

This asshole had to die. And now. I swept my foot out and took him by surprise. Most shifters didn't know martial arts—why would we need it when we can sprout fangs and rip someone's throat out?

Jarod fell forward onto his hands, and I aimed carefully. One shot behind the left ear, and he dropped the rest of the way to the ground, dead.

I tucked the gun back in my pocket and walked around the far side of the diner—opposite of the way we'd arrived—to my truck.

It was for the safety of all shifters, I reminded myself, as I had every time I took a life. There were no shifter prisons. There was no other form of justice besides the council ruling and the enforcers meting out the appropriate punishment. Human justice was for just that: humans. If Jameson had been captured by the FBI, it wouldn't have gone well. A shifter in prison? It wouldn't hold him. He was a danger to the peacekeepers as much as the criminals. On top of that, it would result in our species being revealed.

I acted for all shifters only because someone had to. There were eight enforcers in all of North America. When there was a vacancy, it was filled. When I was nineteen, Rob had approached me, took me to the Shifter Council meeting and offered me the job.

Job. It was more of a role. Council enforcer. There were rules with the task. Secrecy. At the time, I'd been honored. My best friend had been alpha for three years and had authority. His brother had joined the Green Berets to fight for human lives. I'd been young and restless. Eager to prove my worth. I hadn't even imagined the burden ending someone's life would have. The secrecy of it. I did it because it had to be done. Jarod Jameson wouldn't have stopped. And I'd rather it be me than some shifter with a taste for blood. Or someone like my younger brother, who couldn't live with a tainted soul like mine.

I might come across as the quiet one. The peacemaker at the ranch. The calm cowboy.

Little did they fucking know.

In the truck, I poured water over the wound, trying to wash away the silver dust or whatever the tip of the knife had been poisoned with.

The edges of the gash were already pulling away, angry and red, the opposite of how a shifter wound normally behaved.

Fuck.

It would heal, but it would take time. I'd have to hide it from my brother and the rest of the ranch hands. My parents. Even if I got gored by a fucking bull like Boyd had, the wound would heal quickly. I couldn't explain this one away.

Sighing, I started the truck and took off. My job was done. Five hours and I'd be back in Cooper Valley. I could report to Rob and glue the edges of the cut back together with superglue. Colton had said that was something humans did when in a situation where they couldn't stitch a wound although I was sure no shifter had ever tried it. Or had need.

We had a doctor—Audrey—living right on the ranch, but I couldn't even ask her for help. She might be able to stitch me up since the wound was behaving more like I was human than shifter, but she'd know something was up. Boyd's wound from the bull goring had healed before her eyes. She'd seen a teenaged shifter get shot by that fucker Markle. She'd even helped a child at her own wedding reception to know shifters healed differently. She'd question this. Not even her mate knew my role with the council. Hell, I doubted she even knew there was something called an enforcer.

Thinking of the human doctor brought back thoughts of her friend, Becky, the lovely nurse I'd hooked up with at the bachelorette party.

As I drove north on the two-lane road, I imagined Becky's nimble fingers sewing up my wound. Forget about the damn wound, I'd like to see those nimble fingers wrapped around my dick again, tugging hard, asking for a hard fuck. But that wasn't going to happen, and there were several good reasons why.

I sighed, wiping my face, then wincing as lifting my arm tugged on the oozing wound.

A male like me couldn't mate. Not with the role of council enforcer. My job was my life, even if it was a secret. If anyone ever found out, I'd have assholes out for revenge climbing out of the woodwork. I'd heard enough about enforcers and how they were hated for serving justice so ruthlessly. And anonymously. My role was needed—and hated

—among all species of shifters. Because of that, any mate of mine would never be safe.

Becky wasn't mine. She never had been. My wolf didn't recognize her as my mate. She was just a gorgeous human who'd gotten under my skin just as much as this poison in my side. It was taking a long time to heal from a quick encounter in a storage room.

3

ECKY

I PUSHED the cart through the produce section and stopped in front of the avocados. I gave one a gentle squeeze, then another, finding some that weren't too firm or soft. I added a bunch to my cart. I never used to like avocados, even avoiding guacamole at Mexican restaurants as if it were some kind of green slime.

Now? I couldn't get enough of the things, which wasn't helping my bank account. November in Montana wasn't the best time to get them, but my body wanted the dang things, and they stayed down.

At least it was healthy, unlike my ridiculous craving for cocktail wieners.

I'd only thrown up once today, which was a miracle in itself. I worked on the labor and delivery floor at the hospital. I knew all about pregnancy. Well, I thought I had, until I was pregnant myself. My OB assured me that while having morning sickness into my second trimester was perfectly normal, it wasn't fun.

No shit, Sherlock.

It wasn't too severe that I worried about nourishment or being dehydrated. My little peanut gave me a reprieve for most of the day to get food down. And keep it down. The rest of the time? People needed to watch out.

It just seemed like a long time since the nausea began. Since I found out. Even longer since that night. *That night.*

The night that Clint the Hot Cowboy and his super sperm got past a condom and knocked me up. Not only had the wild ride he'd given me in the storage room been a surprise—I'd never had a quickie before in my life—so were the two blue stripes on the pregnancy test I took a few weeks later.

I'd worked at a clinic telling people the

importance of using condoms, that they weren't a foolproof method of birth control.

Again, no shit, Sherlock.

The fateful July party was supposed to have been fun. A little wild. Something for Audrey to remember as a crazy bachelorette party before she tied the knot with her hot rodeo champ, Boyd. She wasn't the only one who wouldn't forget it.

I knew Boyd and Audrey went at it like rabbits. Even back then. *Especially* back then. But they hadn't been the ones to get all hot and heavy in the storage room.

I had. With Clint Tucker. While I'd never met him face-to-face before that night, I'd seen him in passing, and I'd liked what I'd seen a whole hell of a lot. I'd been friends with Audrey since she first moved to town, and we began working together at the hospital. After she met Boyd, I'd gone to the ranch and seen Clint in the corral with the horses. That was when I realized I had a thing for cowboys.

He looked like the Marlboro man without the cigarette. Dark hair, muscular. Big. Well, over a foot taller than me. He had the square jawline and rugged appearance of a manly-man, but there were smile lines around his eyes that made him seem trustworthy.

There had been other guys around, but I'd been snared watching him. Only him. There'd been a calmness about him that was a draw, as if he knew who he was and didn't give a fuck what anyone else thought. At the ranch and at the bar that night.

It was a complete one-eighty from my ex.

If there was a photo of a dick in the dictionary, it wouldn't be of a penis—it would be my soon-to-be ex-husband's face. Todd was a dick. Clint wasn't one, but definitely had one, and look where that got me. Pregnant. I should have learned from Todd and steered clear of men. I had, until Clint and my need to save a horse and ride a cowboy. I had a trusty vibrator, and I should have blown out the motor.

I pushed past the fruit and steered to the meat counter. It was damn hard to eat the amount of protein recommended, according to my doctor's meal sheet. I sighed as I waited for the butcher to come over, so I could order some sausages, but the smell of the raw fish at the far end of the display hit me hard. I gagged before I could even talk myself down.

Oh shit. Where was the bathroom in this place? I spun in a circle, wondering if it was up front by customer service or here in the back, but that only made things worse.

Abandoning my cart, I whirled away from the counter and ran smack into a wall of... tall, hard man.

Big hands wrapped around my elbows. "Hey," a deep, all-too-familiar voice rumbled. "Becky... hey. Wow. Um... hi. Uh, you all right?"

I craned my neck to look up and... into Clint's handsome face. My eyes widened in surprise and panic. His nostrils flared as he drew a deep breath, and for a moment, his startled eyes seemed to change from green to grey. I quickly dropped my analysis of the color of his irises because the act of moving my head too fast brought on another wave of nausea.

"Jesus, you look green," he commented.

For a third time in five minutes, no shit, Sherlock.

I stepped to the left to get around him, but he followed. I shifted to the right as if I were a football tight end trying to get past an opposing linebacker.

"Hey," he said at the same time as I told him to move.

He didn't, and that was it for me. I doubled over, heaving, and—God help me—puked a little on Clint's work boots.

"Oh my God," I croaked, keeping my head down

as I shoved my hand in my purse for a tissue. "Oh God, this is so embarrassing."

I hadn't seen Clint in four months, and now I threw up on him. Because of his baby being all sadistic and torturing me from the inside out.

"You okay? Shelby, get her a bottle of water," Clint barked.

"Yep. Be right back." The sound of a female voice brought my head up again, just in time to see the gorgeous juice bar girl from the farmer's market heading away. I stared at how her snug jeans showed off an ass she could probably bounce a quarter off of. Her short puffy coat didn't hide anything.

My stomach instantly settled. As in a brick sunk in it and held it down.

It wasn't like I was interested in Clint. I wasn't! I hadn't told him there'd been consequences to our hookup a few months ago because the last thing I needed was guy complications. Sure, I'd stewed on that issue for a few weeks. Did I tell him? Did I not? He deserved to know. No, it didn't matter. We'd left it as casual. A quickie. Nothing more.

I had enough trouble trying to get through my divorce from Todd in one piece. We'd been legally separated for two years, but he wouldn't sign the papers. Wouldn't end it. Instead, he wanted to fuck with me. Draw it out. Push up my legal bills in the hopes I'd give up and go back to him.

Yeah, I'd go back to a guy being a dick just to get me back. Todd was dumber than I'd ever thought. I was stuck with him legally until he gave up and just signed.

A wild fuck at the back of Cody's was one thing, but I didn't need some other guy making demands of me. They were nothing but trouble.

That was the whole reason I hadn't gone to Audrey to be my Ob/Gyn. Not only did I not want my BFF to see my vagina or a baby popping out of it —I did have some boundaries in friendships—I was afraid she'd put two and two together and realize who the father was.

Still, seeing Clint with Juice Girl jabbed me with a hot poker of jealousy. Clearly, he and his dick had moved on. I would never have a tight body or even tighter ass. My baby belly and my breasts popped over the last week.

"Let's get you somewhere you can clean up," Clint suggested, looking me over.

Thank God I had on a heavy coat and a bulky sweater beneath.

"I'll just go home," I mumbled, trying to lurch away. To forget this moment ever happened.

But Clint maintained contact with one of my elbows, following along beside me as if I required his strength to walk.

Which would've been nice if I had. Or if I hadn't just barfed all over his feet.

Gah!

Juice Girl materialized out of nowhere. "Here you go—it's already paid for."

Clint snatched it from her hand with a murmured thanks, unscrewed the top and thrust it at me. "Take a sip."

I grabbed it, desperate to escape. "Thanks so much, both of you. I gotta run before I hurl again."

"I'll drive you home," Clint offered.

"No, no, no, no." I couldn't seem to stop my lips from saying the syllable over and over again. "I'm okay on my own."

I was. Completely on my own.

"Probably," he countered. "But I'm not letting you drive yourself home when you're feeling this way. Give me your keys, sugar."

Sugar. He'd called me that at the bar. It had sounded good then and now.

But I wasn't his sugar. He was with Shelby, and I knew he wasn't an asshole, so I had to assume he called every woman sugar. Like the mechanic who worked on my car calling everyone honey.

I looked up at him, my embarrassment morphing into something hot and slithery. My ever-tender nipples beaded up in my now too-tight bra. I'd just thrown up, and I was hot for him. Eager for what he had in his pants. And the dark words out of his mouth.

Clint was bossy.

I shouldn't like that.

Not after Todd's controlling asshole ways. He'd told me what to do, what to wear, what to buy.

But it seemed a girl never learned because Clint's take-charge attitude just erased all nausea and left my panties damp.

I had hormonal whiplash. Nauseated one minute, horny the next.

Yeah, as if Clint wanted to get it on with a woman who just hurled on him. Soooo sexy.

Still, I hesitated. Part of me was anxious to escape, especially considering Clint *was here with another woman.* But he held out his hand and pinned me with that stern dark gaze, and I found myself passing the keys before I'd made up my mind whether to obey.

"What about your groceries?" Clint asked, glancing behind me at my cart.

"I just need to leave," I begged. "I'll come back tomorrow and apologize to the manager."

"Okay. Shelby, would you mind—"

"No problem. I'll take care of our shopping. Give me the keys to your truck, and I'll finish up."

Well.

She was awfully accommodating considering Clint was leaving with another woman. She must really be eager to please. When I glanced at her, I found her eyeing me with curiosity rather than jealousy.

Uh oh. Hopefully they weren't into threesomes.

Oh, what was I thinking? Nobody was thinking about having sex with me right now. I just puked in a grocery store. On a hot cowboy's boots.

He was just being a gentleman and seeing me home.

I let him steer me outside, and I pointed out my Subaru. He opened the passenger door and handed me in like I was some kind of elderly woman then walked around, pushed my seat all the way back and climbed behind the wheel.

"Where to?" he asked, looking over at me.

"Listen, you don't have to drive me." I opened the

Wolf Ranch: Savage

glove box and pulled out some napkins, which I thrust at him. "For your boots."

He took them and leaned down to give his boots a quick swipe. "Thanks. Now, where do you live?"

"I'm really sorry, Clint. I don't want your girlfriend to be mad." I couldn't help myself. I just had to ask. He was a nice guy, and I didn't want to mess things up for him.

"Girlfriend?" He raised both brows in surprise then his lips twitched. "You think Shelby's my girlfriend?" He shook his head and started the car. "No, sugar. She was just helping me pick up some things for a family gathering we're having. It's too cold for a barbeque but same kind of thing."

"Oh. She's—um—family?" Dammit, did I sound way too hopeful? Did I really think a gorgeous guy like him would be single?

He backed up, lips tipping up again. "Yep, we're related. I couldn't tell you exactly how. Second cousins, maybe—I don't know. But yes, she's family."

I sat back, my stomach calm, much of my agitation easing. "Well, she seems really nice."

I liked her far better now that I knew she wasn't Clint's girlfriend. She seemed like a really awesome cousin. Stellar, even.

I gave Clint directions back to the duplex I'd

moved into when I first left Todd and arrived in Cooper Valley. Thanks to the crushing weight of his med school bills—yeah, *his*, not mine—I couldn't afford any better. I still couldn't since we were still fucking married, and his debts were my debts.

"What do you think made you sick?" Clint asked. "Stomach flu? Food poisoning?"

I drew in a breath. "Food poisoning, probably," I said quickly. While Clint might eventually find out I was pregnant, I couldn't deal with the complications that would bring at the moment. I'd wanted to see him again, but I'd wanted to be prepared. Have a mental script of what to say. Heck, even makeup and maybe not have throw-up breath.

As happy as I was that he and Shelby weren't an item, that didn't mean I got to lay claim to him. Or that I even wanted to. His dick would be good, but all of him? All six-feet plus of hot cowboy? I wasn't ready for that or the complications that went with it.

I would have enough problems when Todd found out I was pregnant. Knowing that asshole, he'd probably try to claim paternity even though we hadn't had sex in two years. He was determined to cause me as much trouble and delay our divorce for as long as he possibly could. Adding a pregnancy to the legal proceedings was going to be a nightmare.

"What do you do for that?" He glanced over from the wheel.

Seriously? Had he never had food poisoning before? "Oh, you know. Lots of fluids and staying closer to a bathroom than I did. I'll be fine. I'm already feeling better. Again, I'm sorry about your boots."

"Stop apologizing," he said firmly in that same bossy tone that had made my nipples hard at the store. He pulled in front of my place, parked and quickly texted the address to Shelby, so she could pick him up. He turned to look at me, his gaze roving over my face. "What can I do to help?"

"You've been a huge help already, but it's enough." I opened the door and climbed out, my boots sinking into three-day old snow my neighbor and I still hadn't shoveled.

Clint surged out from behind the wheel and jogged to catch my elbow, like he was afraid I'd slip.

I stopped and smiled at him. He really was quite the gentleman. The memory of him gallantly riding to my rescue the night we hooked up came flooding back with fondness. "I'm fine. Really. Hey, your nose is looking better."

He lifted his free hand to touch it as if he'd forgotten, then grinned. "Yeah. All good."

"Don't worry about me," I replied. "I'm good, too."

"Well, I *am* worried." His forehead crinkled. He steered me forward to my door. "I'm going to come back and check on you."

My heart did a little somersault before I promptly stepped on it.

Nope. Dating Clint was off the table.

Way too complicated, and I knew it was better to steer clear of him from the start because I had a feeling he had a slew of broken hearts in his wake. I didn't want mine to be one of them.

"It's really not necessary."

"Tough. I'm going to come by just the same," he said firmly, tipping his cowboy hat.

I tried to ignore the clenching between my legs that simple act produced while Clint stepped even closer and stared down at me as if fascinated. He took a deep breath as he studied me.

Oh lordy. I wouldn't mind a repeat of the night we hooked up.

It had been mind-blowing to say the least. I remembered the feel of his hands on me, the hard press of his body against mine as he held me pinned to the wall. The feel of him hot and thick between my legs. The deep thrust of his dick. The way he looked when he came. How it felt when he made *me* come.

Shit, I wanted that again. So bad. But I couldn't, even though my vibrator didn't compare. That one night had already gotten me in a world of trouble.

If I weren't worried about barf-breath, I would've stood on my tiptoes and kissed his cheek, but considering my horrific state, I thought it best to simply duck into my place and wave from the door. Shelby had just pulled up in Clint's truck, so I was home free.

"Thanks again," I chirped, trying to close the door in his face.

"You can close the door on me now, sugar, but I'll be by tomorrow to look in on you." He stepped back.

I waved again and shut the door.

Crap.

Resisting that sexy cowboy had been doable today because I'd puked on his boots. Tomorrow would be a different story.

I wasn't sure I had the willpower necessary to resist the magnetic attraction I had to the father of my child.

4

Clint

Mate.

How could I have been so stupid? I'd missed that the hot little nurse was my mate. Four months ago, I'd had my mate in my arms, my dick deep in her pussy, and I'd had no idea. That was one for the shifter record books.

Fuck! A growl rumbled from my chest as I drove out of town.

My nose had been freshly broken the night she and I hooked up at Cody's, and I hadn't been able to smell, but still—shouldn't I have known?

Yeah, I'd been attracted to her from across the

room, but so had lots of other guys. Including the one who'd punched me.

Prickles ran all down my arms, across the back of my neck thinking about it. Becky was my mate, and she'd been alone, unprotected while I'd been away. I hadn't even had any of the other pack members watching out for her. Nothing from me.

Nothing. I was the shittiest mate ever. I wanted to beat the shit out of something, pissed at myself for not being there, even when I'd had no idea. It made leaving her behind now even worse.

I'd breathed in her honeyed scent at the meat counter in the fucking grocery store, and I knew.

My wolf had howled and preened with joy.

She'd been sick! I'd attentively driven her home, ensuring she was safe. What kind of mate left? Walked away when she was clearly feeling poorly?

Me.

As I drove my truck up the mountain to the pack cabin for our meeting, I ignored the curious glances from Shelby, who was probably smart enough to put two and two together. And stay silent.

A wolf didn't get that interested over a human puking in the grocery store for nothing.

Now that I reviewed our interaction at the bachelorette party, all the signs were obvious. How

I'd lost control when that asshole had tried to pick her up. How satisfied I'd been when she'd gone with me into the storage room. How satisfied *she'd* been when we were finished. How I hadn't wanted it to be a one-time thing.

But it had never occurred to me that she might be mine.

Mine.

And now, it had taken all my willpower just to walk away from her and get in my truck when Shelby had pulled up in front of her place. Claiming a human wasn't the same as claiming a she-wolf. They didn't recognize you by scent. They had different ideas about how partnerships with the opposite sex were formed. Becky had no idea she was mine. Even worse, all she probably thought of me was the quickie she'd had at Cody's over the summer.

She wasn't a quickie. Sure, we'd *had* one, and I'd walked away. I'd been gone pretty much the entire time since, dealing with enforcer shit. There had been no opportunity to revisit the connection we'd had. To see if there was more.

It was a coincidence we'd bumped into each other at the store. Coincidence she'd thrown up on me. I'd blocked her path not knowing... fuck, my mate was sick! That was going to torture me all fucking night until I got eyes on her again and could verify she was feeling better.

Yeah, I'd had to leave. It had been obvious she'd wanted me gone, embarrassed at being sick on me. I didn't give a shit about that. I was in this with her, throw up and all. She just didn't know it yet. Like Audrey and Marina before her, she knew nothing about shifters. What I really was. What she meant to me.

Which only had my frustration ratchet up another notch. The further I drove away from her, the angrier my wolf got. I had to figure out what to do because she was fucking mine, and I'd take care of her. In fact, I might need to get a place in town, so I could keep a closer eye on her. Even if she wasn't ready to accept me as her mate, she required protection. Seeing her sick reminded me of just how vulnerable she was.

Protection.

Oh, fuck.

Reality hit me like a brick in the temple.

How could a council enforcer possibly mate? I'd already written it off as a bad idea. I'd gone into the role with my eyes wide open, knowing the danger, the threat to my life. My job had zero rainbows and unicorns. It was all silver bullets and neck snapping.

The assholes I hunted had zero problems with hurting those who I cared about to get back at me. Hell, being mated to an enforcer all but put a bullseye on a female's back. It would be especially bad with a human. She was so vulnerable. One punch from a vengeful shifter could snap her neck. And humans didn't have regeneration capabilities. She would die.

I'd never be able to live with myself if something happened to her.

Hell, I already wouldn't be able to ever sleep again for fear something could happen.

Dammit.

I'd just found my mate, and I couldn't have her. The safest thing for Becky was for me to stay away. Her own mate was her greatest threat.

Fuck!

I pulled in front of the pack cabin and backed around, so the tailgate faced the front porch to unload the supplies for the meeting and dinner afterward. It was a new moon, but I was as agitated as I'd be at a full moon. I smacked my hand on the steering wheel, and Shelby just watched then climbed from the truck.

I slammed the truck door as Rob came out of the building to help. He eyed me, as if he could already sense the shift that had taken place inside me. It was true. I was normally very even-keeled. I was the *quiet one.* It was one of the reasons I'd been chosen to be an enforcer. I was strong and lethal but lacked the blood from an alpha line that produced hot-headedness or the need to prove something.

Colton would have made a good enforcer and proved it in all his years in the military, but he was in line to be alpha. And without a mate, he could've gone moon mad.

I'd volunteered for the job. Dealt with the consequences of it. The danger. The long lapses of time away from home. Even killing.

I'd thought I'd be safe enough from moon madness, not having the alpha line's blood in my veins. Now that I'd met my mate? Now that I knew how hard it was to stay away from her? To not claim her? I wasn't so sure. I'd only known Becky was mine for about an hour, and I was starting to lose my shit. I would go insane if I didn't claim her, moon madness or not.

"What's got into you?" Rob asked as I stomped around the truck, the snow smashing under my feet with a satisfying crunch. He grabbed some of the bags. "Your side bothering you?"

I scowled. My breath came out in a white cloud as I eyed my friend. My alpha.

My side? My head had been so focused on Becky, I'd completely forgotten about the throbbing wound. I wasn't used to healing at such a slow pace, but this wound was a good example of the impact silver had on shifters. It burned and was just starting to close up. It would heal completely over time, in another day or two... but shit.

"It's fine," I grumbled, not used to being coddled about an injury. Hell, it was the only time I ever had one. As a kid, my mother hadn't even done it since we fucking healed so fast. Except for now.

He looked at Shelby who shrugged but said, "I think you Wolf boys aren't the only ones Fate threw together with a human."

Rob stopped mid-stride, five bags of groceries balanced in his arms. He pinned me with a look, eyebrows raised. "That right? You found your mate? Holy shit."

My scowl grew deeper.

"Who is it? Someone you saw in town?" he prodded.

I snatched a bag off the top of Rob's load because

between him and Shelby, they'd already unloaded everything. I chose to ignore them both as I stomped inside.

I hadn't gotten it sorted in my head yet. The last thing I needed was to talk it over with my alpha.

"Hey, Clint," Willow, Rob's mate, called from the kitchen. Shelby had been wrong about Willow being human—we all had. Turned out the DEA agent possessed latent shifter genes that presented themselves when her life had been threatened by a bullet to the gut. She'd shifted for the very first time at the age of twenty-six, her inner wolf coming out to save her. While Rob had accepted Willow as his mate when he'd assumed she was human, our alpha had actually mated a rare and beautiful ginger wolf.

I dropped the grocery bag on the counter.

"I'm going for a run," I muttered, not waiting for Rob or Shelby.

Wolves didn't normally run during the day when the chance of being spotted by a human was higher, but we were up on the mountain, on pack grounds. I'd be safe enough. I was an enforcer. I knew the fucking rules, and they included not mating. Sure, they were *my* fucking rules. My job was dangerous. What kind of mate was I who killed as ordered? A mercenary. An assassin. Sure, I only finished off rogue shifters who needed to be put down, but still. There was a darkness in me that would taint Becky. Destroy her as it would surely begin to destroy me.

I really, really needed to let off some steam; otherwise, I'd be in my truck and headed back to my human mate, and that was the last thing I could do.

Hey, sugar. I'm your mate. Yeah, I'm a wolf shifter, and I'm going to bite your neck as I take you hard and make you mine forever. Oh yeah, I'm a council enforcer who ends rogue shifters with a silver bullet to the brain. Let's fuck.

I stripped and shifted to my wolf, with fur as black as my soul, I knew that wasn't going to work. Not one fucking bit.

5

Becky

Well, crap on a cracker.

After tugging my mitten off with my teeth, I pulled out my cell from my purse and called in to work. As it rang, I took in the snow that had fallen overnight. Not much, but enough to add another inch to the last round. It was flipping cold out, and I stomped my booted feet on the driveway as I stared at my car.

"Talia, hey, it's Becky," I said when a fellow nurse answered in the labor and delivery department. "Look, I've got a flat tire, and I'm going to be late."

My driver's side tire had been slashed. It had been obvious when I'd come down the walk, seeing the car off kilter, and even more obvious when the cut was on the side wall. No nail ever punctured that part.

I needed only one guess who'd done it. Todd, my deranged ex.

Yes, Todd. Slashing my tires will definitely make me come back to you.

"That sucks," she replied. "Don't worry. It's quiet now. Only one patient, only four centimeters dilated, so you're good."

I sighed in relief, my breath coming out in a white cloud. "I'll be there as soon as I can."

I hung up, tucked my phone away and went around to the trunk to find the jack and the spare. There was no way I was driving anywhere right now, and no way I could afford a tow truck to help.

I stomped my foot on the ground again, this time in total frustration. Why couldn't Todd just leave me alone? Sign the fucking papers and move on with his life? What guy wanted to be with a woman who didn't want to be with him?

I'd met Todd when I'd worked as a nurse in the ICU at a hospital in Billings. It had been my second job out of school. I'd been warned about dating a doctor, but I'd fallen for Todd's attention and charm. He'd been sweet even. Told me everything I wanted to hear. Growing up with parents who considered me their *accident,* I'd craved love. Looking back, it was so obvious how desperate I'd been. How stupid. But Todd had been good, though. Manipulative. Twisted. Cutting me off from friends, deciding which shifts I worked. Hell, even which department I worked in. Little by little, he'd chipped away at my independence.

I hadn't even noticed as it happened, adapting as best I could to keep him happy. In love with me. Until he hit me. Only once. Sure, it was a dick move, but I was actually thankful for it. It was literally the slap in the face I needed to wake up and catch on to the shitshow that was my life.

He'd gone out to drink after blaming me for making him angry enough to hit me. I'd quickly packed my car with whatever I could fit and left him that night. I'd gone to an attorney, got divorce papers started.

Almost two years later, I lived two towns over and on my own, yet I was in the same fucking situation. Still married to the asshole who refused to sign. Who went before the judge and threw out all kinds of shit to drag it out. To drag out the costly expense for my lawyer. At this point, I had no doubt my bills would be putting her son through college.

I huffed and kicked the flat tire as I thought about having to pay for Todd's school loans. Being married still meant being legally tied to Todd's debts. It had been one thing to float him as he finished his residency while I worked, but another to pay his bills now when we hadn't lived together for years.

"Fucker," I muttered. I hadn't seen him in months, not since the last court visit when I had to argue that the new granite countertops he'd had installed at his house, *in my name,* were not my financial responsibility.

And now this.

I put the jack under the car and managed to pump it until the carriage lifted enough for me to get the wheel off the ground. Then I put the lug wrench on one of the lug nuts and turned it counter-clockwise. Correction. I *tried* to turn the damn thing counter-clockwise, but it literally wouldn't budge. It was hard to grip with my mittens on, and I wasn't strong enough to get it to move. Not even an inch.

I was sweating beneath my heavy winter gear from the strain.

I ignored the sound of a car pulling up the street. I'd never been one to play a helpless female. Yeah, a decent guy would stop if they saw a woman trying to change a tire. Especially in this small Montana town. But I wasn't going to flag someone down or anything. I could figure this out on my own. I was used to dealing with shit by myself.

The car stopped, even though I didn't think I was visible from the road. I heard a door slam and the sound of a heavy pair of boots packing down the snow. I peeked around the side of the car, and my heart skipped a little.

Clint. All six feet plus of him.

My sexy cowboy was here to check up on me. No, not *my* sexy cowboy. Just *a* super sexy, bossy, sexually potent and skilled, cowboy. He had on sturdy leather work boots, jeans and a thick coat. He wore his cowboy hat, even in twenty-degree weather. His hands were bare, and I doubted he felt the least bit cold. I was sweating now for an entirely different reason.

It was his dark stare that took in every inch of me that had me licking my lips.

He might have the most impeccable timing imaginable. If I wasn't happy to see him because of it, I'd wonder why he was here in the first place.

He was quick on the uptake because he was already taking in my tire with narrowed eyes.

I cleared my throat. "Hey. What are you—"

"Someone *slashed* that?" he barked, cutting me off. Like he was pissed off. No, more like he was going to kill someone over it.

It immediately reminded me of the punch he'd taken to the nose at Cody's. How he hadn't even winced when he'd been hit or when I'd set it later. He hadn't even shown anger, really. He'd just delivered his form of justice—swift and sure—by lifting the loser by his neck right off his feet which showed how strong Clint was. Unusual. Most guys would have decked a guy right back. But no, Clint had just shown the guy his strength. The potential for harm. He left my would-be suitor practically scrambling home to his mama.

"Yep," I said, standing up and setting my hand on the car window since I was lightheaded. Fuck, for a second there, I'd forgotten I was pregnant. I hadn't been nauseated yet this morning. Shit. I shouldn't have been doing the stupid tire.

"Any idea who did this?" he asked, looking around as if Todd lurked behind the bushes.

It was tempting to tell him everything. Maybe unleash that protective streak he seemed to have for me, having him go all Incredible Hulk on Todd. Boy, that would have been awesome.

But no.

That would complicate things even more. If I thought Todd was making my life hell now, I could only imagine what he'd do if he thought I was dating someone. He still considered me *his,* and getting a guy into the mix, even one as big and brawny and who could clearly take care of himself as Clint, was just stupid. I had no idea what kind of spin Todd would put on it before a judge. I was already desperate to get our divorce finished before he discovered I was pregnant.

I shrugged. "Probably some neighborhood kids."

He cocked his head, searching my face like he didn't believe me, but then took the tire iron from my hand. He stood so close I could feel the heat radiating off him. He brushed his finger over my cheek. "Go wait inside where it's warm. I'll get this changed for you and get you on your way."

That bossiness again.

I didn't know why it was so damn sexy coming from him. It was the complete opposite of Todd who was manipulative. A gas-lighter. Always making me feel like I screwed up and needed to scramble to fix my mistakes.

Clint hadn't suggested I couldn't fix the tire on my own, only said he'd do it for me. Somehow, he made me feel like I was perfect, and he'd take care of everything.

I wasn't sure he'd still think that if and when he found out I hid my pregnancy from him. *Our* pregnancy. God, that sounded strange.

I let him nudge me toward my door and went inside, taking the opportunity to get some more food in me before I got queasy. That was the trick with morning sickness—never let your stomach get empty. It was counter-intuitive because I'd learned the hard way once I felt sick, I sure as hell didn't want to eat anything, but eating down the nausea was the only thing that worked.

I kept a sleeve of crackers in my purse at all times, but since I was still at home, I fixed myself a second piece of toast with avocado mashed on top. When I wasn't nauseated, I was ready to eat for ten. I had a feeling it was only going to get worse.

I ate the toast quickly, but it wasn't quick enough because a knock at the door indicated Clint was already done. I swore that guy was so manly he made the Marlboro Man look weak.

I threw open the door just as he was about to knock again.

"All set," he said. His gaze raked over me in my pink scrubs beneath my opened coat. "You'll have to get a new set of tires for the front. I called Bishop's, and they should be able to hook you up this morning if you have time to stop there now on your way to work."

Two new tires. Yay! Not.

"Thanks, I do," I said calmly. It wasn't his fault I was wasting my money on things I shouldn't even need. "I really appreciate your help. It was really nice of you to stop."

He stood in the doorway and watched as I zipped up my coat and grabbed my purse then locked up. I followed him out to my car.

"Guess you must be feeling better," he said, turning to face me, like he wanted to make small talk. Like he didn't want me to leave.

Oh God, this guy. I wished he wasn't so damn sweet, not that I'd tell him that to his face.

I glanced up at him and smiled. He smiled back. Oh shit, was that a dimple in his scruffy cheek? My stomach flip flopped and not from morning sickness. What was he doing hanging with me when he had a hot grocery-store-shopping girlfriend? No, she was family, but there were hot, single women all over Cooper Valley eager to nab a hot cowboy like him.

"Much better," I said when I realized he was

waiting for a response instead of me staring at him. "Promise not to puke on you today. So how was your, um, family thing, that you went to with your *cousin?*"

A slow grin spread across his face. "Shelby. My cousin, yes." We stood beside my car. He advanced, like a hunter stalking his prey, backing me against my door and caging me in. One hand was on the roof, the other at my hip over my thick coat.

"You weren't—you know—a little bit jealous when you thought she was my girlfriend, were you?" A dark brow winged up as he waited.

I let out an exaggerated *pfft* and stared at his Adam's apple. Even that was manly. "What?" I blinked, and I knew my cheeks turned bright pink. I could feel the heat of it in the frigid air. "No. I mean, you and I… we hooked up one time, months ago. Of course, you've had other women since."

Oh God. Why was I prying into this? I really, really didn't want to hear the answer because if there were others just as pretty as Shelby, I might have to crawl back in bed and throw the covers over my head for… forever.

He shook his head slowly, a little smirk playing on his lips. I remembered how those lips had felt against mine, how he kissed. Wild. Potent. God, he'd been as into it as I had that night.

Okay, maybe I did want to hear. I had to know.

"No one?" Those two words sounded way too hopeful.

His face moved closer to mine until our lips were centimeters apart. I heard him take a deep breath and... growled?

"No one," he swore. He smelled of cinnamon and a scent I remembered as... Clint. Some kind of soap because he wasn't the kind of guy who wore—or needed—cologne.

My nipples hardened beneath all my layers as if my body remembered him.

I wasn't going to kiss him. I definitely had a plan to actively avoid doing anything resembling kissing with Clint. I had a plan to actively avoid *Clint,* but that wasn't working.

I stared at that mouth. "Then you haven't... with anyone... since we—"

"Nope."

With that one word from his lips, I went up on my tiptoes. That was all it took for my lips to encounter his. As if the devil himself was pushing me up with a nudge from Hell.

And, oh damn, a kiss never felt so good. Because

the moment I made contact, Clint took over, kissing me aggressively, plowing his tall, firm body into mine and pressing me against the car. One of his thighs slid between mine, and I rocked my pubis down on it, finding friction for my clit as he slanted his mouth with a searing intensity.

I had no idea how long we made out in my driveway, but I was sure all the snow around us had melted by the heat we were putting off.

"Clint!" The startled cry came out of my mouth when we broke apart, our breathing ragged.

I may have initiated, but hell, I'd surprised myself, and then, he'd surprised me even more with his response.

Damn, did we have chemistry. We might be the *definition* of chemistry.

But no matter how wet that kiss made my panties, getting involved with Clint would be a major, major complication right now.

And the pregnancy muddled things too much. When I'd decided not to tell him about the baby, it was because I never really expected to see him again. But twice in less than twenty-four hours was proving I'd been stupid. And the kiss? He'd been just as into it as I was. That was a *really* big problem.

Now, not telling him about the baby made me out to be... a total bitch.

But I didn't want to rush into a new relationship when I hadn't signed the papers on the old one. Sure, the stupid divorce had been in the works for *years,* so it wasn't rushing, but it wasn't over. The tire proved it. I still had to deal with Todd.

On paper, I was married!

When Clint learned I was pregnant with his child? Well, he seemed like the kind of guy who'd want to "do right by me and the baby" and marry me before I gave birth. Just like with my parents. I'd been an accident and so was the baby I carried. I refused to be an obligation. He wouldn't want me to have a bastard. He'd probably be all chivalrous and save my reputation or some old-fashioned crap like that. That was what made my parents' lives miserable.

One thing I knew for sure—I wasn't rushing into marriage again. And definitely not for the wrong reasons. Not even with a guy as hot and dick-skilled as Clint.

The longer I stood here with my lips tingling from Clint's kisses and the need to beg for more of them, the worse this was going to get.

"Clint, listen." I set my hand on his chest. His

rock hard, broad chest. *Bad move!* "I really like you—a lot."

His brow furrowed, wariness replacing the lust I'd seen there a moment ago.

I rushed on before I could take the words back. Because God only knew, I didn't want to say them. "We obviously share a mutual attraction."

He frowned.

"But I'm married."

Clint reared back as if I'd punched him. *"What?"*

I glanced around to see if his roar brought out the neighbors. The word sliced through me like a hot wire, leaving me in two pieces—the one piece that desperately wanted to take my words back and the other that knew this was the right thing to do.

I swallowed. "Separated two years ago but still legally married," I explained because I didn't want him to think I was a cheater. "I'm not... not an adulterer. I'd have been divorced eighteen months ago if Todd hadn't blocked all my petitions."

I looked down at the wet driveway. It almost hurt to see the look on his face now.

"So, you see, I'm not really in a position to enter a relationship or keep kissing you. Whatever you want to label it. It's just... bad timing for me."

When he didn't say anything for a long time, I

glanced up. His expression changed to stormy. "Bad timing," he repeated, taking another step back. His hands clenched into fists then released. Over and over. I didn't get the impression he was trying not to punch me, but it seemed like he was holding himself back from grabbing me. Holding me close. "Definitely."

I swallowed the urge to apologize. Sorry wasn't going to fix this—it just was what it was.

I'd done the right thing. We couldn't get involved now. My life and world were far too complicated, and Todd was going to continue to ruin everything. I had to wonder if I was divorced now, if Todd had signed, if I wouldn't push Clint away. If I would tell him about the baby. Too many ifs.

As Clint tipped his cowboy hat at me and walked to his truck, I knew the answer would be yes. I felt the strange urge to cry at the loss of something that never really got started.

That was the hormones talking.

It wasn't real.

Just like this thing between me and Clint could never be real.

6

Clint

Married.

Fucking married?

I waited until I'd turned off her street before I demolished my dash with a smash of my fist. The wound at my side throbbed, as if in direct response to my agitation. Fucking hell. The burn was a reminder of exactly what I'd intended to do. Not go after Becky. But I had, and in the end, she'd given me the perfect excuse *not* to do so.

Then why was I fucking losing my shit? Fate was *a cunt*.

I seriously wanted to kill someone right now, and I wouldn't have minded if it was her husband.

Soon to be ex-husband, I hoped.

I never touched a married or claimed woman. Ever. She didn't belong to me.

But Becky did, though. My wolf didn't care about a legal piece of paper. A marriage was a human bond, not a shifter one. The fact that she'd ended it two years earlier meant she wasn't *with* her ex. She was fair game.

To me, the man, it fucking blowed. I couldn't mate a married human!

No matter how much my wolf wanted to turn around and keep on kissing her, I drove straight to the ranch and shot off an email to the council data-digger, some hacker who lived in Arizona. I might have pretended it had to do with shifter enforcement rather than my mate's marital status, but I had to know everything about Becky Nichols, and this was the easiest way to do it.

She got back to me in thirty minutes—thank fuck.

What I read both infuriated and appeased me.

Becky's been separated for two years—just as she'd said—following an incident that resulted in a restraining order being filed and a legal status of separated.

A prickle of fear ran up my spine at that. The only kind of *incidents* that required a restraining order were ones where someone was in danger.

I growled, stood and tossed my chair across the room. Pacing the small space, I thought about how my mate had been hurt by her husband. She'd had to file papers to keep him away. She'd said he wouldn't sign, that he'd blocked all her petitions. Still. Two fucking years later.

God fucking dammit. I was seriously going to kill the asshole.

I froze, realizing I'd been a big fucking idiot. Standing in her driveway, it had been right in front of my face. Hell, I'd replaced the fucking thing.

The tire.

Could her ex have slashed her tire? He lived in Meade, about thirty miles away. It seemed beneath a —I skimmed the data for what type of doctor the ex was—gastroenterologist to drive to the next town over just to slash his wife's tire, but it also seemed beneath a doctor to hit his wife.

Violence wasn't reserved for blue-collar workers, was it?

It happened in every society and every type of

household. He might have driven her to file for divorce, but since it still wasn't final, it didn't seem like he was inclined to let her go. He was fucking with her from afar. Or right in her driveway.

Goddammit! For the second time that day, I slammed my fist down and cracked the recipient of my force—this time my desk.

I took a deep breath and let it out. Another, but wished I could still breathe in her sweet scent, not the lemon cleaner that had been used in the room recently. Fixing the chair, I settled back at the computer and kept reading the information the data-hacker sent. Becky had filed for divorce two years ago, but Dr. Todd Nichols used various legal delay tactics to block a final divorce decree from being filed. At issue seemed to be their large debt and how it would be divided up.

I opened another email. Attachments showed a house in Meade had a sizable mortgage, and liens from several home improvement contractors were filed on it. The loan was in both spouses' names, but I couldn't miss a bill for kitchen renovations completed six months ago in Becky's name.

Only her name.

Which meant the douche canoe was using her to pay for shit she didn't even know about. I wasn't up on the legalities of marriage in Montana. Hell, never had I imagined I'd be mated to a human, let alone consider marrying one. Unless Becky's lawyer was a complete moron, the law had to be in Todd's favor, meaning Becky would be liable for the new kitchen solely because they were still wed.

There was more. Lots more. All indicating that Becky was being fucked over by her husband.

I leaned back in the chair, tossed my hat off and ran my hands over my face. Shame filled me. I'd added to her shit by walking away. By freaking the fuck out over what she'd said. She'd been honest and as upfront as she could be.

During the night at Cody's, it wasn't as if either of us were in the right mind to talk about anything beyond a condom being used. Sure, she'd been married, but legally separated and in the middle of a divorce. She'd had every right for a fun fuck. She'd also had every right not to tell me about her ex.

A slow smile spread across my face. Becky shared that little gem with me now because she wanted *more* than a quickie. We'd been standing beside the evidence of her ex's latest dick move. He'd been right there at the forefront of her thoughts. She told me the truth, all of it, because she wanted me to know the truth, know what she was up against.

That meant she wanted me. I'd do more than change a fucking tire for her. I'd finish her ex, so she didn't have to spend a second stressing about him ever again. That was my job as her mate, to protect her in all ways.

I stood, grinned. My wolf howled and circled, eager to get back to her. To pull her into my arms and tell her everything was going to be fine. That she was safe. That her ex was going down. She had a fucking council enforcer to take care of her. Fuck, yes!

Wait. Fuck, no.

She needed protection, but it couldn't be from me. I was a fucking council enforcer. I dealt with rogue shifters not human assholes. I wasn't even allowed to mess with the guy, not only because he was human but because it would give away my job and the fact that I had it and shifters in general.

Audrey and Marina were both human, and while I was sure they'd been stunned to learn shifters even existed, they'd embraced it. They were part of the pack now. Audrey was even pregnant with the start of the next generation of Wolf pups. Rob had allowed the match. Hell, he'd gone so far as to go after a human female of his own, but she'd turned out to be half-shifter.

Still, Boyd, Colton and Rob weren't enforcers. They didn't have shifter blood on their hands like I did. They didn't have their purpose within the pack kept a secret.

What the fuck was I going to do? I couldn't stay away knowing what I did about Becky's ex. Not when I'd gotten a whiff of her scent again and confirmation from my wolf that she was mine.

I had to talk to Rob, the only one within the Wolf pack who knew the whole truth about me. I had to figure this shit out and soon. It might have been just a tire today, but what would be next?

7

Becky

"I'm sorry, ma'am. This card has been denied."

After waiting an hour in Bishop's small waiting area for the tires to be replaced, the scent of old coffee and motor oil making my stomach queasy then desperate for forbidden caffeine. I was hungry and tired and cranky. Mostly cranky. While I'd played a stupid game on my phone, my thoughts had veered to Clint.

Why had he come by? He lived on the other side of the mountains at Wolf Ranch. It made no sense why he was on my street unless to see me. Had he driven over twenty miles just for me?

His kiss said yes. His response to the bomb that I was married not so much. Well, maybe even more so. It didn't matter though. It was over. *Very* over. No honorable guy messed around with a married woman. Clint *was* honorable. I knew it. He might be a dirty-talking horndog, but when his dick wasn't hard, he was a nice guy. I hadn't had time to prove that, but I just knew.

No way would he be friends with any of the Wolf brothers otherwise.

"I'm sorry, what?" I asked, blinking at the guy.

"Denied." He held up the credit card and offered me an expression that screamed *whoops!*

After all this, the card machine was clearly broken. I hadn't made it into work yet and would have to work over lunch to make up the lost time.

"Could you try it again please?" I asked, starting to feel panicked.

He gave me a sympathetic smile. "I did. Twice."

He handed me the card.

"Twice?"

He nodded.

There was no reason for the card to be turned down. I paid my bill in full each month because I didn't like to be in debt. At least, not in debt more than I already was being tied to Todd. The tires would eat into my budget, but I'd be able to pay for them if I watched my pennies this month.

I offered him a small smile and held up a finger. "I'll be right back."

Moving to stand in the corner of the small shop's waiting area, I called the number on the back of the card. After pushing a whole bunch of numbers to get me to a customer service representative, the person finally told me that my husband shut off my card the day before.

My husband.

Bile rose in my throat at what Todd was now doing. Not only had he slashed my tire, he'd shut off my card, so I couldn't pay for it. As my *husband*, he was able to do so. I just had no idea how he'd gotten the card number. It was a new card. I'd signed up for it after I'd left him.

I glanced out the plate glass window and down Main Street. There hadn't been enough snow for the streets to need plowing, but there were big piles of it from the last storm. I saw the bank the next block down, and my blood ran cold. If he could get to my credit card, he could—

Dashing over to the desk, I shoved the small

amount of cash in my wallet I had at the mechanic. "Here. This is good faith. I'll be back to pay you. Keep the car. I have to run to the bank."

I didn't wait for him to reply but bolted out the door and down the street, my boots splashing through the small puddles. Thankfully, Cooper Valley was tiny, and most stores and businesses were within blocks of each other. I burst through the bank's entrance with a gust of cold wind and definite dread.

It took ten minutes to learn that Todd had withdrawn all the money in my personal checking account, and I was, in fact, overdrawn since my electricity bill was set to auto-pay.

While the bank teller hadn't done anything wrong, in fact, she'd been following the law, she looked really upset about my situation. Her pity only made me want to cry. I wanted to scream. I wanted to rip my hair out. I wanted to rip Todd's head off and shove it up his tiny ass.

I went out onto the sidewalk because there was nothing else the bank could do for me. I'd checked to see if Todd had an account, wanting to take his money out like he had done with mine. But no. Of course not.

The cold breeze raced down the street. I didn't

care. I was already numb. Before Todd got another dime of my money, I called human resources at the hospital and explained the situation and asked them to immediately switch my paycheck off of direct deposit. If I had to hide cash in a can in the backyard, that was what I'd do to keep it away from Todd.

In order to get the money, I had to make it, which meant I had to get my ass to work. I walked back to the mechanic, trying to think about how I was going to pay him all the while hoping he'd be kind enough to drop me off at the hospital.

When I cut across the street, I stopped at the curb. Stared... then blinked. Leaning against a shiny black Mercedes was Todd. His arms were crossed, and he was smiling at me. He wasn't quite six feet tall and had a slim build. He had a personal trainer although any money he spent was wasted since he didn't look the least bit fit. On his feet were his signature loafers, even in the crappy weather. And his car... how the hell was it so shiny after the storm and the sloppy roads?

I looked like hell, having only eaten the avocado toast earlier. I was in my scrubs, my hair pulled back in a ponytail beneath my knit hat.

Maybe it was the pregnancy hormones. Maybe

it was because he was a total fucking asshole, but I lost it. He'd stolen money from me. Money I needed to pay rent. Electricity. Food. He didn't give a shit. No, he did. He gave a shit that I left, and he was forcing me to come back to him by bleeding me dry.

"What the fuck is wrong with you?" I screamed, waving my arms and approaching Todd, getting in his face. I hadn't seen him in months, not since the last court visit, and that had been with lawyers present. And a judge.

"What's the matter, honey?" His eyebrow rose in mock confusion.

"You know what's the matter. You stole money from my bank account. You cancelled my credit card!" I practically shook with fury.

He frowned. "How could I steal from my own wife? It's not *your* money. It's *our* money."

It was possible the top of my head blew off then and there. There was no *our*.

"Ma'am, is everything all right?" The mechanic must have come out when I started shouting. Bless his heart for checking on me, but there was nothing he could do for the hurt Todd had already caused me.

"My wife is being irrational. I will take her

home." He reached out to take my arm, but I wrenched it away.

"We are legally separated," I snapped. "We'd be divorced if you just signed the fucking papers."

"Language, honey," he said in a patronizing tone.

"I have a restraining order for you to stay away from me."

He held up his hands as if I was the one who'd messed with him. "You're the one who approached me. How was I to know you'd be here?"

"You slashed my tire, asshole. That's how you knew I'd be here. You're a dead man, Todd. Dead. You've fucked with me for the last time."

I spun on my heel and stormed off, not waiting to ask the mechanic for a ride. I doubted he'd give one to a lunatic like me, especially after the ridiculous threats I'd spouted. Several other people were watching my little tantrum, but I didn't care. I was done. D-O-N-E.

I wanted to cry, but I was too angry. I knew I would, later, when the adrenaline wore off.

As I walked the mile to the hospital, I ate the crackers from my purse. The entire sleeve of them. I would normally have been freezing on the way, but I had my anger to keep me warm. I had no idea what the fuck I was going to do. Todd wouldn't stop until

I gave in, and that was the last thing I would ever do. I wasn't going back to him. I saw him for what he was now.

Insane and perhaps even dangerous.

It wasn't just me I had to worry about now. It was little peanut, too. I wouldn't let Todd get anywhere near my child. It was only so long, though, that thick sweaters and heavy coats would hide my growing belly. If he was this crazy now, what would it be like when he found out I was having another man's baby? Where would he stop? Slashed tire and empty bank account today. What would he do tomorrow?

8

Clint

I COULDN'T SLEEP. There was no fucking way I could while thinking about seeing Becky fix her own flat tire. Not just flat. Slashed. I'd respected her request that I leave, but that didn't mean I was abandoning her. Hell no. Space, she got. She also got me, and I was going to figure out what the hell was up with her ex. It was how I could protect her. For now.

I researched the fuck out of Becky's and Todd's case into the night. In Helena, there was a shifter who was a lawyer and a damn good one. Selena Jennings. She was the kind of attorney humans paid eight hundred dollars an hour for. I said *humans* because she usually did her work for her own kind *pro bono*, not that I wouldn't be willing to pay her. I'd pay her anything to make Becky happy, and I had a feeling that would start when the ink was dry on her divorce papers.

I put in a call to her to ask if she would look into Becky's situation.

"Does Becky want my help with her divorce?" she asked. "Has she fired her own attorney?"

I cleared my throat. "No."

I heard her huff out a laugh. "She doesn't know you called me, right?"

"She's my *mate*," I growled. "She's in danger. This man is tormenting her. He slashed her tire, I'm sure of it. It can't be the first thing he's done, and I doubt it'll be the last."

Selena sighed. "I understand, but there's not much I can do without her willingly becoming my client. Do you have access to any of the paperwork?"

"I have it all right here pulled up on my laptop," I replied, mentally thanking Kylie, council data-hacker for getting me everything.

"Send it over, and I'll take a look," she said with resignation in her voice.

I sighed in relief. "Thank you. Appreciate it." I hung up and forwarded everything onto her then rubbed the back of my neck, my continued unease making my wolf growl. There was nothing I could do to nudge Selena along except harass her, which would piss her off. That was the last thing I wanted. I had to be patient, but it was fucking tough when something still felt off, even after getting someone on the legal end of things.

It was a feeling I couldn't shove away. I stood, paced. Something was wrong, and my wolf was telling me. I had no idea what the fuck it was, but it had to be acted on. I grabbed my coat. Christ, I needed to move into town. I didn't like being so far away from my mate's house. Twenty miles from her was too fucking far. And if she was in danger... *fuck*.

I didn't have an invitation. In fact, Becky had downright pushed me away this morning with her marriage announcement, but I had to go look in on her. Just drive by to make sure the sense of foreboding I had wasn't about her. It was my gut talking. My Spidey sense as some people said. Whatever it was, it had saved me a time or two when tracking a rogue shifter. I wasn't working now, which made it even worse.

I got in my truck and drove into town, cruising down Becky's street at two miles an hour. It had been dark for hours, and this time of year, people settled inside at dinnertime and stayed in. Cars were in their driveways, the streetlights were on. In a few weeks, the front yards would be glowing with holiday lights.

Nothing appeared off, yet the sense of unease got stronger even though her house was dark except for a porch light. I glanced around once more. The snow made the night brighter, not that I needed it with my shifter vision. There were no new cars parked around—I'd taken note of all of them that morning when I'd been by.

I stepped on the brakes, hard, right in front of her place.

The fuck?

A shadow moved under her window. A figure. I threw the truck in park, right in the middle of the street and flew out of my seat.

"Hey!" I barked, stalking toward the fucker.

I didn't know what I expected. For the guy to run, maybe. That I'd scare him away with my voice before I got there with my fists.

"What the fuck are you doing?"

The asshole just swiveled and stared at me, like he belonged there, under her window, looking in.

A light went on in the room where the guy was peeking, and the shades parted. Becky looked out her window and screamed. It was muffled by the glass, but I sure as fuck heard it.

Don't kill him. Don't kill him. Don't kill him.

I had to keep reminding myself because I was a hair's breadth away from shifting to tear the guy's throat out.

Some rational part of my brain remained, telling me to cool my jets. To follow the code and not betray my species to humans. Not to harm a human. I was on a quiet street in Cooper Valley—not the place for a wolf to appear. Especially not one who was ripping out a guy's throat. That couldn't be explained away.

Oh fates, but I wanted to.

Becky yelled through the window. "Todd! You asshole. I'm calling the cops right now."

Todd. I wasn't sure if I was relieved it was her asshole ex or not. It only proved what I'd told Selena. The guy wasn't done with Becky.

I was proud of my woman, keeping her shit and getting on the horn with the police. I made my way over to him, my feet crunching through the snow at the side of her house. I'd hold him until they got here. The fucker wasn't getting away on my watch. This was trespassing and whatever the fuck the law was for being a Peeping Tom. I was on him in seconds, my fist wrapped in his jacket to bunch it into a ball as I shoved him back against the house, hard.

His head connected with the windowpane, and he yelped.

That made my wolf howl, so did the twinge from the healing wound in my side. It was taking fucking forever to go away.

"Ow! Who the fuck are you?"

I got right in his face. "I'm the guy who's about to fuck you up, creeper." Despite my obsessive need to publicly claim Becky, something told me not to show my hand with her ex just yet. To let him think I was just some guy driving by.

Not her fucking wolf mate ready to rip him to shreds with my teeth.

"I'm her husband!" Todd protested, eyes wide. "I was just checking to make sure the windows were locked."

Becky came barreling out the door in a pair of boots and a coat thrown over her pajamas.

"Bullshit!" she snapped from the porch, peering into the darkness toward us. "He's my ex, and I have a restraining order against him."

The only thing that kept me from savaging Todd

was the fact that Becky sounded more angry than scared.

I dragged Todd away from the window and closer to the porch light, so she could see my face. Know I was here to keep her safe, to take the trash out. My wolf preened as I watched recognition and relief bloom in her expression. The way those berry lips parted and uttered my name did a lot to calm my wolf. Yeah, she might've pushed me away, not once but twice, but she trusted me and knew she was safe. I'd walked away this morning, but I wasn't doing it again.

Of course, it brought Todd to a rage. "You know this guy?" he snarled, his smugness falling away.

"I know everyone in this town," she snapped.

Ouch.

Even though I figured she didn't want to share our relationship with him, it still stung to hear her downplay what we were.

At least I fucking hoped that was downplay and not the way she thought of me. Although, to her, I was a guy she fucked at a bar one night over the summer, who'd randomly run into her again. The kiss we'd shared at her car should have been a big fucking clue that we weren't done, even to a human.

Becky held up her phone. "The sheriff is on his

way, asshole. And he's not going to buy your checking the locks on the windows story."

"I'm checking up on my *wife*," he tossed at her. "Making sure she's safe while she chooses to live apart from me."

Becky rolled her eyes and crossed her arms over her chest. "You are so full of shit. What was this really? More vandalism or were you actually trying to crawl through my bedroom window, you sick psychopath?"

Todd didn't like that. He lunged for her, and I snarled, slamming him up against the house, my fingers wrapped around his throat. It would be so easy to watch the life drain from him. The evil would die, and my mate would be free of him. But then, she'd see the real me, and I couldn't allow that. Ever.

9

Clint

"Clint," Becky warned immediately, like she was afraid I would take things too far. She wasn't wrong. It was my job to eliminate rogue shifters. Well, this fucker was a rogue human.

Fuck, she might be right. My jaw was clenched, and my gaze was narrowed. I had no doubt my eyes had changed color. This dickwad wasn't just harassing Becky, he was *flaunting* it, as if it was his right.

I was usually level-headed, but when it came to her, I lost all control.

I squeezed harder for another few beats then

released my hold on his throat and watched him slump against the side of the house and cough.

"You like to beat on women?" I asked, pulling him up, then slamming him up against it again. "Huh? Is that why she had to file a restraining order?"

"She's my *wife*," he shouted, like that made everything okay.

Becky was right. The guy was a psychopath. He certainly didn't seem to have a healthy grasp on reality or that Becky wanted shit to do with him.

Except—and this would have been comical if it wasn't fucking wrong—the moment the sheriff parked and approached, Todd shifted into playing the injured party. As the lawman listened, he was just the smooth-talking, concerned husband checking on his wife.

I went over to Becky, resisting my desperate urge to make contact even though I wanted to wrap my arm around her and pull her in close. Instead, I stood at her shoulder with my arms folded across my chest, like her fucking bodyguard.

Which I was—or planned to be. Among other things. Up until now, she didn't know it. But now? Everything had fucking changed. There was no more of her pushing away. There was no more of me giving her space. Her ex wasn't just a jerk. He was a problem to her safety. The way she was shaking, to her health, too. I couldn't step back a second longer.

A second patrol car came, and between the two officers, Becky's restraining order was checked out. Once he caught on that neither man was going to fall for his shit, he got quiet. Fast. Todd was arrested and taken away as we watched. Little did the guy know, he was safer in jail since I couldn't get my hands on him.

I'd have to talk with Rob. As alpha, he heard issues like mine. My mate was being threatened, and the cause had to be eliminated. It was the pack way. The challenge? Todd Nichols was human. We couldn't make a doctor from Meade disappear. It was my job to see things like this done. The one time I was eager to kill someone, I wasn't able to do it.

After the cop cars' brake lights disappeared around the corner, I turned to Becky and set my hands on her shoulders. So she didn't have to wrench her neck, I bent down, so we were eye to eye. "You okay?"

She nodded. "Thanks for helping. Do you want to come in for… coffee or something?"

If coffee was a euphemism for headboard banging sex, then yes.

"I'll come in, sugar, but just for you to pack a bag."

She frowned.

"You're not staying here. Not when that fucker's still breathing."

She laughed. "I foresee him breathing for a very long time. I'd just like to not be legally tied to him. Although, killing him has crossed my mind."

I turned her toward her front door and nudged her inside. She'd been outside in the cold long enough. "Sugar, I don't blame you. Now, let's get a bag and get out of here. You've probably had a long day, and you should get some sleep."

I followed and closed the door behind me. She flipped a switch and a lamp gave the living room a soft glow. Her place was small but cozy. A tan couch faced a gas fireplace with a flat screen TV above it. It was clearly a rental with cream walls and neutral carpet, but landscape photos on the wall gave it some personality.

"I'm not going with you." She rested a hip against the back of the couch.

"You're not staying here." No fucking way. She didn't know she was mine, and I had to get her to see it, slowly. But not in this house and not alone.

She sighed. "I've dealt with Todd for two years. Longer when we were truly married."

"Two years is long enough," I countered. "Pack a bag. I don't want you anywhere that asshole can find you. End of story." I stepped into her personal space, dropping a hand to her hip. She felt soft and warm beneath my palm, and at the simple touch, my wolf popped up and sniffed.

I heard her breath catch as she gazed up at me and licked her lips. "You do bossy really well, but that doesn't mean I'm going to do what you say. We had fun. One night. That's all."

I arched a brow. "That's all? I've been hard since we kissed this morning."

Her gaze dropped to the front of my pants, which only made my dick swell even more. I took a deep breath. Yeah, just as I thought. "You're wet, aren't you? For what I can give you."

She huffed as if she was infuriated, but I couldn't miss the way her cheeks flushed or her pupils dilated. Or her scent. My wolf practically howled at the sweet scent of her pussy.

She *was* wet, and if I got my hand in those pajama pants...

"You're cocky, too."

I grinned at that and cupped myself. "You liked

cocky once. I'm ready for another go, but a bed would be good."

She blushed a deeper shade of pink. "Cocky. Bossy. Whatever. It's all the same."

We weren't getting anywhere, and I wanted to be somewhere safe, not still here in her living room. I always meant what I said, and she was not staying in this place alone. It had been practically painful walking away from her not once but twice knowing she was mine. I wasn't doing it again.

I had no idea what the fuck I was doing, but I knew she wasn't remaining alone. Even if I couldn't claim her, my protective streak told me to keep her safe.

"Bossy, huh?" I finally said. "You wanna see bossy? I'll show you bossy, sugar." I tucked my shoulder into the crease of her hip and lifted her into a fireman's carry, bringing her into her bedroom. "This is me carrying you home with me. I'm not leaving here without you, so you'd better start cooperating and pack a bag." I gave her butt a light slap, and she laughed.

I tipped her onto the bed and followed her body down, pinning her beneath me. I gathered her wrists above her head. "Either I'm staying here with you tonight, or you're coming with me now. But you're not sleeping anywhere alone again, and that's my final word."

"I could call the cops on you, too, Clint Tucker." Her broad smile belied her threat.

I nipped her neck. "I wouldn't try it if I were you."

She squirmed beneath me, rolling her hips to meet mine. My cock hardened painfully against my zipper.

"He's in jail. Todd won't bother me tonight."

I growled as I stripped her of her heavy coat, tossed it onto the floor.

"Tonight. Something tells me he won't be in there for long." Slippery fuckers like Todd weaseled their way out of shit. Being a respected doctor in the next town over was in his favor. And I had no doubt this incident would only piss him off. He'd be back.

Her face fell as she considered my words. She knew I was right but didn't say anything. She knew him better than I did, knew that nothing had stopped him in two years.

"Are you going to take me all the way out to Wolf Ranch?"

Well, I hadn't thought that through yet. I slept in the bunkhouse with the other ranch hands. Getting my own place had never been important to me because I hadn't had a mate.

But it sure as hell was now.

Getting thrown up on in the grocery store had changed my entire life. That chance encounter had let me discover what I'd had right in front of my face… right on my dick without even knowing.

My parents had a place in town they used as a vacation rental, and that would serve. They didn't rent it this time of year, for there wasn't much demand in comparison to the summer months. "I know a place we can stay where your creeper ex won't find you. Come on." I forced myself to roll off her—because I had her exactly where I wanted her—and pulled her to her feet. "I'll help you pack. You can ditch the PJs though. You won't be needing them. If you get cold, I'll keep you warm."

10

Becky

"We're not having sex," I blurted as Clint ushered me out to his truck with a hand at my low back, my suitcase in his other hand.

I was dying to have sex with him. Especially when I'd just had all six feet of hard body covering mine on the bed, but if we got naked, he might notice my baby bump, and then complications would become problems.

I had enough of those. My, hopefully, soon-to-be-ex husband had just been outside my bedroom window. I was obviously in no position to get involved with someone new, even if that someone was the father of my unborn child.

Especially because that someone was the father of my child.

I was being cruel, I knew, but God, I couldn't be stuck with Clint out of pity or because we'd had an epic contraceptive fail. Thanks to my parents, I knew what being stuck with a guy was like, and while Clint was nothing like Todd, I refused to be trapped to any guy for the next eighteen years… hell, the rest of my life, without love.

"Okay," he said mildly. "No sex. I just need to know you're safe."

Damn.

Why did I just say no sex? I was nuts. I knew pregnancy brain was real, but what woman, pregnant or otherwise, would skip any kind of sexy shenanigans with a hottie like Clint? His protective streak alone made me wet. My tender breasts practically throbbed for him under my jacket, and my panties had been damp since the moment he threw me over his shoulder and carried me to the bedroom. Take into account his cowboy swagger, his dark intensity or his ability to deal with Todd with only one hand, and I was a horny mess. I didn't dare remember how his big dick had felt when he'd taken me hard against the storage room wall at Cody's.

Or how swoony I found it that he demanded I spend the night under his protection. He was truly concerned about me, and that was worst of all because it made my heart melt just a tad.

He helped me up into the cab of the truck and walked around to the driver's side. The air was frigid, sharp and crisp, but I barely noticed. I looked over at his rugged profile as he started the truck.

"So... what happened tonight?" I asked. "I mean, how did you happen by my street at ten at night?"

He rubbed the back of his neck. "I just had a bad feeling," he said, stealing a look at me as he drove. "I pay attention to my gut when it tells me something's wrong."

As if I hadn't already thought he was a badass. Now I found out he has a sixth sense thing, too.

"I swear I'm not stalking you." The corner of his mouth quirked. "Although I guess it looks that way."

It did seem it, but nothing about Clint made me nervous. I felt... safe. With Todd, I was always on edge, even when he was charming. I always felt off-balance and wrong-footed, as if I could never say or do the right thing. With Clint, it was the opposite. I felt totally at ease. There was even the looming issue of my pregnancy standing between us, and I was going off with him into the cold night. The cab of his truck was warm with the heat blasting.

He pulled up in front of a cute cottage not far from Audrey's house in town. "This is a place that my parents own. It's not rented right now, so you can stay here as long as you need."

The porch light was on, and the sidewalk shoveled. A large tree was in the front yard, and I guessed it was leafy and shady in the summer. It was… cute.

"Thank you for this," I reached over and touched his arm. "I've been alone in this mess with Todd for so long… it feels nice to have someone in my corner for a change. After what he did today, I admit it felt good watching you try to strangle him."

He frowned. "You're talking about more than the tire, aren't you?"

I looked away, nodded.

Fingers beneath my chin had me looking back at him. "What else did he do?" The question was low and deadly.

I took a deep breath, told him about the credit card and the bank account.

"Fuck… shit, sorry."

I laughed at the way he tried not to swear. The

feeling, the... lightness of being with Clint was almost foreign to me.

Easy.

He took off his hat, ran a hand through his hair. I realized I'd never seen him without his cowboy hat before. His dark hair was longer on the top than the sides. It *had* been groomed until his frustration messed it up. It still looked good.

"Sugar, I'm definitely in your corner," Clint declared. "Even without sex." He threw open his door.

"Yeah, about that..." I slid out my side of the truck and dropped to the ground.

"Oh?" There was no denying the obvious interest in his voice. He pulled my suitcase out of the back seat and walked around to meet me.

"I might have been a little hasty," I admitted. God, I'd made it five whole minutes after telling him no sex to *yes sex*. I was a little slut where he was concerned.

His eyes caught the streetlight and for a moment looked like they glowed silver. His grin was definitely feral. I didn't even know how it was possible because he was still holding my suitcase, but he somehow swept me up into his arms like a new bride and carried me up to the doorstep. I gasped and set my hand against his hard chest. Even without a coat he was warm.

Hot, even. Literally and figuratively.

"There's no pressure, sugar," he said in a deep, velvety rumble. "I need to keep you safe, that's all." He fit the key in the lock and pushed the door open. "But if you did want a repeat of our previous escapade, I promise I'll make it worth your while."

The bastard winked. Of course, the wink was my undoing. I bit his neck. He growled.

"Make you a deal," I whispered.

"All right." He flipped on the lights. I shot my hand out and flicked them back off.

"Keep the lights off, and I'm all yours."

He stood still for a moment. I couldn't make out much of his face in the darkness, but his eyes still glinted, almost like an animal's. Like he could see in the deep shadows of the room. But of course, that would be impossible.

"Deal," he murmured, carrying me swiftly through the darkness, like he knew his way blind. He kicked open a door and lay me on a soft bed. I tugged off my coat and heard the thunk thunk of his boots hitting the floor. I toed mine off, too, then pulled my pajama top over my head.

This was going to work out perfectly.

Wolf Ranch: Savage

He wouldn't see my baby bump, and I'd still get to have fun. It wasn't like we'd seen much of each other in the storeroom. My skirt had been hitched up about my waist, and he'd been too frantic to do more than yank my panties to the side. I'd barely gotten a glimpse of his dick. We'd had incredible sex without seeing each other's bodies. We could do that again now.

In the back of my mind, I knew my reasoning was about as wonky as a tilt-a-whirl, but I ignored my better sense. I blamed it on the hormones. I'd never been hornier in my life than I had been since I started growing this baby, and the fact that it was Clint here with me...

I had to admit, he'd featured prominently in all my fantasies when I took the time to relieve my frustration with my fingers or my battery-operated boyfriend since the summer. He'd pretty much ruined me for all other guys.

I cupped my tender breasts, my nipples already hardened into tight buds.

Clint stilled then inhaled, as if he could see what I was doing, but that was impossible. The room was so dark, I could barely make out his outline. I heard the rustle of his clothing and tried to conjure an image of him stark naked.

I remembered from our night together he was made of solid muscle. Ripped abs beneath my palms so defined you could climb them. A long, lean frame. Thick, over-sized dick.

"Sugar, if you want the lights out because you're embarrassed about some part of your body, can I just tell you right now that you're perfect?" he rumbled, his voice coming closer. I felt the dip of the bed and imagined him setting a knee down and crawling toward me.

Oh yeah, I was totally prey.

I shimmied out of my pajama pants. I wasn't wearing panties because, well, I was an Ob/Gyn nurse, and I knew the importance of getting air down there. I also knew the importance of more than one form of birth control.

"It's not that," I said, but my hand went to my baby bump. "I just feel more comfortable this way. Okay?"

"Sure. This time." His gravelly voice hummed right beside my ear, and he pushed me onto my back, covering my naked body with his.

I shivered, relishing the shock of hot skin on skin. Clint nipped and licked down my neck to arrive at one nipple.

He flicked his tongue over it, cupping and

squeezing my breast the way I'd just been doing. "You're bigger than before," he observed before taking my nipple into his mouth and sucking.

The corresponding tug between my legs made me arch up with a gasp. "Oh shit, Clint. Y-you can't possibly remember," I argued.

"Oh, I remember," he swore, his breath fanning my sensitive flesh. "Nothing could ever make me forget the sight of those beautiful breasts bouncing while I gave it to you hard in that storeroom. I hadn't even gotten your top off. Now, these gorgeous tits are all mine. I'm gonna give them the attention they deserve."

A streak of excitement ran through me at his dirty talk. And the fact that he was dirty talking about me. My body.

While I didn't want him to guess the true nature of the growing size of my breasts, it felt amazing to be really seen. He'd paid attention. Remembered.

It was unbelievably hot.

He shifted to give the same treatment to my other breast. I shivered and moaned. My nipples were so damn sensitive these days, but he wasn't too rough with them. It was perfect. So perfect, I could've come from nipple sucking alone.

I ran my hands down his sides and around the

back to sink my fingernails in the tight muscles of his ass, pulling his hips tighter into the cradle of my legs.

When he thrust in response, the head of his dick managed to find my entrance without assistance. "Oh damn, sugar," he muttered. "You're already wet for me, aren't you?"

He started to retreat, but I pulled his hips in again, causing him to sink into my greedy channel. I moaned.

"Fuck, Becky. You feel so good. Oh fates...*wait.* Hang on—I didn't get suited up."

"It's okay," I blurted, without thinking it through. It wasn't like I could get pregnant a second time. That horse was so far out of the barn.

This morning, he'd said he hadn't been with anyone since me, so I figured he was clean.

"I'm on the pill," I said to explain myself.

He was already rocking into me, deeper and deeper, as if he couldn't help himself.

"And I'm clean," I added.

"I'm clean, too," he said, sounding almost winded. Or pained. "Fuck, Becky. I've never done it raw. *Goddamn.*" He shoved deeper, a harder thrust. When my head slid toward the headboard, he grasped my nape and pushed me back down then melded his lips to mine in a hot kiss. There was no fumbling in the dark. He seemed to know where my body was in space. All his moves were sure and confident. He was a God in bed and out of it.

He was big, and I felt stretched. It didn't hurt, but my body had to adjust to all of him. The feel of him on top of me, his heavy weight kept off as he rested on his forearms, made me feel totally claimed. He wasn't holding me down, the only thing connecting us was his dick deep inside me, but I felt pinned.

Safe. The way he made me feel... my vibrator was going to be tossed out after this. There was no comparison to Clint's dick. It was as if he knew just how to swivel his hips to hit sensitive spots inside me and to rub against my eager clit.

I kissed him back, rocking my hips to meet his thrusts. How was it possible this guy hadn't already been snatched up? Especially in a small town like this one? He was perfect in every way.

For one glimmer of a moment, I let myself indulge in the fantasy of keeping Clint. Telling him about the baby and signing on with him to raise our child together. But I knew from experience these things didn't work out. Life was far from perfect. Messy. I'd be a fool to rush into another hot mess when I wasn't out of my first one yet.

The darkness made it easy for me to let go of my thoughts and misgivings. To tune into the delicious sensations and do nothing but feel. Clint filling me, stretching me. His rough rhythm. Our ragged breathing. It became more than sex. It was an act of worship—on both our parts. I had this crazy sense that we were meant to be, like there was some god orchestrating everything, and our two souls were meant to collide, meant to dance together.

"Fuck, sugar," he breathed against my neck. He was just as into this.

Something burst in my chest because I realized it must mean our child was meant to be. Perhaps the little peanut had orchestrated everything. The baby's soul somehow threw us together to make sure it would come into this world to the right parents, at the right time.

This was all crazy. Fantasy fiction. I'd been reading too many *Harry Potter* novels. Hell, I was delirious from the need to come.

Except I swore the Earth tilted, and the bed slid sideways as Clint brought the pad of his thumb to my clit and rubbed.

I screamed, arching up as my toes curled up, and my legs shot long alongside him. The orgasm rocked through me like a sonic blast, and I shivered from head to toe as the waves kept rolling and rolling. I'd never come like this before. Not with any other guy. Not with my vibrator or fingers. Not even in the storeroom our first time.

My eyes rolled back in my head, and lights danced in my vision.

And then I was on my belly, Clint nudging my legs wide and entering me from behind. I straightened my arms and braced myself against the headboard, so he could use some force, and he did, setting one hand on my shoulder to hold me in place. He fucked me hard, wrapping a fist in my hair and gently tugging to lift my head.

The sound of flesh slapping flesh, our ragged breaths filled the air.

"Aw, you just got so wet, sugar. You like having your hair pulled?"

Did I? No one had ever done it before.

I whimpered my assent. I sure liked it when *he* did it, anyway. But then, I liked everything he did. Somehow, he'd mastered the art of being both respectful and dirty at the same time. I felt safe with him, even with his huge size and strength. He was fucking me like I was a two-dollar hooker, and yet he was making sure I was right there with him. I was. I so… fucking was.

I felt the headboard lean as he moved his hand and braced against it, too, and he plowed deeper, right into my g-spot. His loins slapped my ass, activating every pleasure center. My swollen breasts rubbed over the bedcovers, my pussy gushed with arousal. I wanted it. Needed it, and I'd already come once. I rarely came more than one time, but this time, nothing was going to stop it.

"Clint," I started whimpering, my need for release getting close again.

"Becky… sugar… I'm going to come," he warned. "I'm going to fill you up."

"Oh God, yes," I moaned, so ready.

He pounded into me, and I arched my back, spread my legs wide and braced my arms to take every wild thrust. This was more intense than the time in the storeroom. Wild. Frantic. As if we couldn't get enough. It was… savage. Both of us were.

"Please," I whimpered, even though it was already happening. I was out of my mind—didn't know what I was saying. I reached between my legs, touched my clit. It was so big, so hard and swollen. "Please, Clint, please."

"Yes!" he roared. "Fuck, yes!" He was a wild beast, pounding over me in a capturing, violent hug from behind. His arms banded around me, and we bounced on the bed and rolled to the side, while he continued to jerk and come inside me.

I swore I felt the heat of his cum hitting my inner walls, searing me with his essence. If I wasn't already pregnant, that would have done it.

"Ouch!" I startled when something sharp pricked my shoulder.

Clint jerked so hard both our bodies lifted into the air and flopped back down on the mattress like we were on a trampoline. "Oh, shit, Becky, I think I bit you." He sounded a little panicked.

"I *know* you did," I laughed ruefully. "I felt it." I reached up to cover the place that stung and throbbed. "Oh my God, I think it's bleeding."

"I know, I'm sorry. Shit, I'm so sorry." Clint moved my hand and—to my shock—licked the place his tooth had punctured my skin. The throbbing immediately eased.

"Seriously. I don't even know how that's possible." I tried to imagine how his teeth could be so sharp because he hadn't bitten me that hard.

"You felt so good," he groaned, trying to catch his breath. "I lost control. I will never bite you again, I promise."

"It's okay," I murmured, already sleepy after the

two orgasms. The idea of him getting that turned on, that kinky, that he wanted to bite me, well, was over the top. Knowing I made him that wild filled me with female power. "I'm fine."

"Fuck," Clint whispered, but he settled behind me, curling his larger body around mine and wrapping an arm over my waist. He splayed his palm right over my abdomen, like he knew about the pregnancy. Like he was laying claim to the baby. Or protecting it.

But that was silly. He couldn't know because it was dark, and I'd covered his hand with mine, so he wouldn't slide it around and explore the shape of my belly.

As I drifted off to sleep, I heard myself humming contentedly, my voice mimicking the pleasure in my body. The warmth in my limbs. The satisfaction of feeling Clint's cum leaking from my slit as he held me in his arms and brushed his lips in my hair.

For now, I was happy. Safe. Sated. The rest? It wasn't going away, but it could wait.

11

CLINT

I marked my mate!

My wolf was off the fucking rails.

Now, as the first morning light filtered through the windows, he was just as content as could be because as far as he was concerned, I was right where I was supposed to be. My mate was sleeping in my arms. My cum had dried between her legs. My scent was permanently embedded in her skin to mark her as mine. No one could doubt who she belonged to now.

My pup grew in her belly.

Yeah, she kind of missed telling me about that.

If things weren't so damn precarious between us —if she understood that she now belonged to me for the rest of her sweet life—I'd turn her over my knee and spank her juicy ass for keeping her pregnancy a secret.

Keep the lights off, and I'm all yours.

Had she really thought she could hide it from me? Of course, she didn't know I could see in the dark. Even if I couldn't, I would've known her breasts were bigger. More sensitive. Her belly had grown, and her pussy had been practically dripping for dick. Her hormones were out of control, and I was the only one who could ease her need. And mine.

Knowing she had my pup in her made me crazed. The fucking had been intense, as if I were trying to give her everything I'd saved up during our months apart.

Hell, if I'd known she was pregnant, I'd have given up the enforcer job months ago. I hadn't known I had a mate *or* a pup on the way.

As she slept soundly in my hold, I had to wonder how long she planned to keep the existence of our pup from me? *How long?*

She'd have to tell me eventually. Winter clothes and heavy coats hid how she grew with my child, but before long, it couldn't be kept a secret. And naked and in the light of day? I'd see it. What then?

Hell, we'd run into each other at the grocery store by accident.

I paused, realized she'd thrown up because she was pregnant. How much more of a sign could I have gotten? Four months, and she hadn't gotten in touch with me. She was friends with Audrey. They worked together, and she could have gotten my number at any time. But she hadn't.

A piece of me was angry, but when I considered the shitshow her marriage had been and the state of her life right now, I could easily see how she might not be in a hurry to open up dialogue with a near stranger about the fact that they'd conceived a child. In the storeroom of a bar.

Maybe she was in denial about the pregnancy. I didn't mean she didn't know. Hell, she'd vomited on my shoes. She knew.

Audrey hadn't said anything about it, and since the night I hooked up with Becky, I'd definitely paid attention when Audrey was around in case she mentioned her friend. I'd been away though, so maybe she knew and was keeping her close friend's confidence.

Or, maybe she hadn't even told Audrey yet.

Audrey was a doctor though. An Ob/Gyn. It was her job to know this shit. For some reason, that thought comforted me. Like I wasn't the only one in the dark. The only one Becky had shut out.

Fuck, I wasn't a woman. I had no clue about these things. I did know we'd used a condom, and it hadn't broken. I felt virile, fucking potent knowing my swimmers still got in.

I smiled to myself. I had a mate... and a child.

I was Becky's mate, and I knew every nuance of her body, and it was different now. Because of me. Because of the baby we made. A prickle raced across the back of my neck. The night before, Todd had lied out his ass and said he was checking on his wife. He hadn't mentioned a kid. Maybe she didn't want her ex to know.

She might be worried this would further complicate her legal proceedings with the divorce. But then, she'd have to certify to the judge she wasn't pregnant—it was part of the paperwork. I only knew that because I'd found what she'd filed over a year ago and read through it. She'd checked the box that said she wasn't pregnant. At the time, she hadn't been.

Yeah, if the asshole found out she was pregnant

with another man's child, he was going to lose his shit. Worse than he already was.

She stirred beside me, and I propped my head on my hand and watched, not wanting to miss a single thing about the way she woke. Her eyes blinked open and met mine. They were soft and open at first, like waking in my arms was the most natural thing in the world to her. I saw the moment her mind caught up. She reached for the sheet and yanked it to her chin, rolling away from me.

"Uh uh." I eased her to her back and slowly lowered the sheet, holding her gaze. She clung to it for a moment, but I persisted until I had it down by her waist. I didn't speak at first. We definitely had things to talk about—big things, and I didn't even plan to touch the *I'm a shifter, and when I bit you, I claimed you as my forever mate* issue—but first I needed to show my reverence for her beauty. The gift of her body and the gift of the sweet pup she was growing.

I trailed the backs of my fingers along the side of her plump breast, down her ribs. I turned my fingers over and lightly brushed over the swell of her lower belly. "You have something to tell me, sugar?" I asked softly to take any sting out of the accusation.

Her pulse went frantic at her throat, and she

abruptly tried to roll away again, but I caught her and dragged her back against my front, my arm wrapped snugly around her waist. I cupped her breast. "You didn't think I'd notice the changes in your beautiful body?"

I felt her heart pound under my palm and through her back, pressed against my chest. I thumbed her nipple which went instantly hard. She sucked in a breath. Fuck, she was sensitive to my touch.

"Aren't you going to ask if it's yours?" she asked in a strangled voice. Her shoulders were tense, like she was bracing for my anger.

"I know it's mine," I said.

I couldn't say for sure, but it didn't matter. If that pup was mine or some other guy's, I'd bitten her last night. I'd be protecting her and the pup until the day I died. Once a male wolf claimed a she-wolf—or in this case, a human female—there was no stopping him from the need to protect and provide for his mate.

That was going to be a huge fucking problem, considering my role with the council. It was why I'd walked away twice in the past few days. What was done was done, and there wasn't any going back. If I hadn't bitten her, the baby bound me to her just the same. I hadn't meant to mark her, but my wolf had driven me to it. It had been just too good between us, especially knowing about the baby. He couldn't stand for our pregnant mate to remain unmarked. He'd lasted all of ten minutes.

We had a lot to figure out.

She rolled over, her gaze searching my face. "I'm sorry I didn't tell—"

I cut her off with a shake of my head. "I forgive you." I gently pinched her nipple between my thumb and forefinger, applying a little pressure and watching her to see what she liked these days. When I added a little tug, she gasped. "Sensitive?"

She nodded as I continued to play.

"Might have to punish you later for keeping it a secret, though." I gave her a wicked grin to let her know it would be the kind of punishment she would enjoy. "I bet we can be... inventive."

Her hips rolled against mine and pupils dilated.

Good. That turned her on. Noted.

"Were you ever going to tell me?" I wasn't sure I wanted to hear the answer to this question. I probably shouldn't have asked it.

The way her gaze slid sideways told me enough.

"Never mind," I said. I definitely didn't want to know.

She drew a breath. "Clint, my life is really complicated right now. I mean, you saw what happened last night with Todd, and you don't even know half of it. I like you—I really do—but we barely know each other. I don't want to, I mean, I *can't* be stuck with you just because we made a baby. My parents did that with me. I was an accident, and they married because of me. They pretty much hate each other."

She raised a good point. A good *human* point. Humans didn't know their life partners just by scent. Hell, I couldn't imagine how much of a pain straight up dating would be to find compatibility. It hadn't worked out for Becky so far, so I couldn't blame her for being skittish now. Especially if she'd had shitty parents to model.

"You aren't an accident," I told her. "Fuck, sugar."

But I was sure. Completely positive we were lifemates. My wolf had scented her and knew. I knew. I'd bitten her and claimed her. I doubted any of that would be good to share right about now. She didn't want to be forced into a relationship because of a baby. I doubted she'd want to know when I bit her last night, she'd become mine, permanently.

She didn't have a shifter mindset, and I definitely needed to keep what I was a secret. For now. I wanted her in my arms, not running away screaming.

I'd done it the shifter way last night. She was bound to me. My wolf was happy, and I was confident she was mine. I'd play it human for her.

"Your ex is an asshole. I'm keeping you safe. No arguments. That doesn't mean we can't get to know each other at the same time. What do you say we get some breakfast and then head to the ranch? There's a new foal you'll probably like."

Her stomach rumbled. Loudly. We laughed.

"It's better than being nauseated," she said.

"Have you been sick much?" I wondered.

She rolled her eyes. "Pretty much from the very beginning."

"I'm sorry I wasn't there for you," I murmured, caressing her tiny bump. I couldn't believe the curve meant my child was in there. "I've been away for work. I'd have come back if I'd known."

She shook her head. "I know. I see that now. Got any avocados?"

I frowned at the change of subject.

"Avocados?"

Smiling, she sat up, and I got a front row view of her gorgeous body. I was going to like those full tits. My mouth watered to suck on them some more, but my woman was hungry, and I would take care of her needs. All of them.

"I've got some wild cravings."

"Don't have any avocados or anything else here, but we can go pick up whatever food you're craving. Me? I've got a craving, too. Your pussy." I lowered my hand to cup her, to feel my cum still slipping from her.

"Oh," she said, and I lifted my gaze to her face.

"I... I have a doctor's appointment at ten. Ultrasound."

My eyes widened, and my hand stilled. "To see the baby?"

She laughed. "Yes, we can even learn the sex. Do you want to know what we're having?"

We. She'd said it not once but twice. This was *our* baby now.

12

Becky

A GIRL. Holy fuck, we were having a girl. I'd thought of the baby inside of me as a peanut, not as a boy or girl. But now? I saw a mental pink explosion. I stared down at the ultrasound image in my lap. We were in Clint's truck, and he sat in the driver's seat staring out the window. I'd never seen anyone go pale like he had when the tech had told us what we were having.

He'd dropped into a chair as he stared at the monitor with our baby on it. It looked like a black and white alien inside a big black circle. It had a big head, legs and arms. It was our baby, who didn't have a penis. Which meant she was a girl.

A girl!

All Clint had said since the announcement was *fuck* over and over.

I bit my lip and glanced at him. He was in big trouble if he was freaking out about having a girl now. He hadn't seen more than an ultrasound of her. When she came, he was going to lose his shit. I doubted he would let anyone near her. He was going to be a protective bear. God, when she started dating… I wondered how many shotguns he owned.

He also had lots of male friends. Big, brawny cowboys who lived on a ranch, who were the overprotective sort. Audrey and Boyd had decided to let the sex of their baby be a surprise, so Boyd wasn't losing his shit like Clint was. Yet. If they had a girl though…

"I'd like to see the foal," I said, trying to snap him out of his thoughts. Maybe it would distract him. Maybe, or maybe he'd be catatonic until she went to college.

I hadn't been sick all morning, and it was almost lunchtime, and I still felt fine. I didn't dare hope I was past the morning sickness in general, but I could take a moment to appreciate my calm stomach. I felt almost human.

"Fuck," Clint whispered, his gaze still affixed at the road.

"How old is it?" I asked, wondering after the age of the foal.

He didn't reply.

"I'm thinking of having sex with the college football team after lunch."

He blinked. That hadn't gotten through either. "Fuck."

I tried not to smile. I really did. "I'm not wearing any panties."

He blinked again, this time looking my way. "What?"

"Have you heard anything I've said since you found out what we're having? Do you even remember walking to your truck?"

He ran a hand over his face. "Fuck."

I laughed. "Clint. A girl's not scary."

His lips thinned. "A girl is fragile. We should have a boy first who can protect her."

"First?" When he didn't respond, I went on. "Not all girls are fragile. Some are tomboys who like to ride horses and catch frogs."

"Not by herself she won't," he countered.

I rolled my eyes.

"Did you roll your eyes at me, woman?"

I rolled them again.

"Wait until my parents hear about this," he muttered. "My mother's going to be cooking you her lasagna every day."

My stomach grumbled at that.

He glanced down at my belly although it was well hidden beneath my coat. He might not have even remembered, but he'd zipped it up for me in the medical center lobby. "Hungry, sugar?"

"Me and our girl want some of that lasagna. Think your parents will like me?"

He took off his hat and sat it on my head. Grinned. "Like you? They're going to forget I'm even in the room when we show up. Let's go surprise them with the news." He turned the truck on then muttered, "Fuck."

CLINT

I'D CALLED my mother from the car, asking her if I could bring a friend for lunch and if she'd put one of her famous lasagnas in the oven. There was usually one ready to go in the fridge for some pack function at all times since it was Rob's favorite dish—the alpha—so I knew I wouldn't be putting her out. Especially when she learned of the reason for the spontaneous visit.

"I assume you didn't say who was coming on purpose," Becky said as we started through the canyon out of town.

I flicked her a glance but kept my eyes on the windy road. The roads were dry, but this was where the Wolf parents had been killed in an accident. I had precious cargo now, so I lightened my foot on the accelerator.

"This is the kind of thing to share in person, don't you think?" I asked.

I loved my parents and saw them several times a week. We were close. It was a surprise, even for me, to have a mate and a baby on the way all in the matter of the two days. It wasn't easy to explain. Becky wasn't a woman I shared on a phone call.

"Sugar, I've barely processed the fact that we're having a girl."

When I'd looked at the ultrasound monitor, I'd had no idea what I'd been looking at. The tech had been patient and talked us through it all. When she turned a dial and the sound of a hummingbird-fast heartbeat filled the room, Becky had started to cry. I didn't, only because I was a big brawny man. Still though, it hit all the fucking feels. We'd made that little thing. I'd leaned over Becky where she reclined on the exam table and kissed her.

When the tech told us the sex... I almost fainted dead away. A girl. I never in a million years imagined I'd ever have a daughter. Hell, I'd never imagined having kids, let alone a mate.

Fate fucked even someone like me and was laughing. Hard.

A girl.

I hadn't been lying when I'd said girls were fragile. They needed protecting from... everything. If I was insanely protective of Becky, I'd probably go ballistic about a daughter.

She'd cry little toddler tears, and I'd give her anything she wanted. She'd get in a fight on the playground, and I'd have to punch some little shit. She'd go to prom and... fuck no. That was never happening.

I'd known we were having a girl for all of thirty minutes, and I was turning insane. Who needed moon madness when there were baby girls to put you down?

Becky began to fidget then pulled down the visor to look in the mirror.

"Relax, they're going to love you."

I took her hand, set it on my thigh. Love her? Holy shit, Mom was going to freak. She'd hinted at wanting grandpups, but she knew that finding a mate wasn't easy. Neither of my parents put pressure on me or Rand, but I had a feeling they would be claiming Boyd and Audrey's child as a grandpup, blood or not. Now they'd have a granddaughter to dote on.

If they watched her closely, didn't let her fall and get hurt. Didn't feed her too many sweets. Kept her warm with mittens and a hat and—

Fuck!

Twenty minutes later, I parked in front of my parents' cabin in the woods. It was about a mile from the main ranch house, set up in the mountains. They'd chosen this spot after they were first mated, and I'd grown up here. The cabin, at first, had been small, but additions had been built on for additional bedrooms and space.

"It's beautiful," Becky said, as she looked out the window at the log home.

"Thanks. Wait there, and I'll help you out."

I hopped out, snow crunching beneath my boots. Up here, there were several inches on the ground.

I opened Becky's door and took her hand. "Careful, it might be slippery," I said, when she stood beside me. "Fuck that."

No way was she slipping, so I picked her up and carried her up the walk to the front door.

"You can't carry me for the next five months," she commented.

"Watch me," I replied. Opening the front door, warm air and the scent of garlic and tomato sauce hit me. It smelled like home, but I realized that *home* was in my arms, and we'd make a place just like this for ourselves. Soon. Hell, very soon if we only had five months. No fucking way were Becky and the baby staying in the bunk house.

My mom came out of the kitchen, wiping her hands on a dish towel and stopped in place when she saw us. "Well. *Hello.*" Her eyes shone with wonder as she looked from my face to Becky's.

I tipped Becky gently back to her feet. "Mom, this is Becky. We're having a baby. Becky, my mom, Janet."

Mom stared and stared. She raised two kids, me and my younger brother, Rand. When Mr. and Mrs. Wolf passed away, she'd pretty much taken in Boyd,

Colton and Rob. Five boys in total. The stuff we'd done should have made her hair white, but she'd taken it all in stride. But this?

I'd surprised the hell out of her.

"Wh-what?" My mom was strong as anything, so I didn't expect her to burst into tears as she rushed to engulf Becky in a hug. "Oh fates, really? You're going to give me a grandbaby?" I watched her breathe in Becky's scent, picking up all the clues. That Becky was human. And I'd marked her.

My dad came into the room, looking on in confusion, but with a smile on his face.

"Dad, this is Becky," I said again. "I admit, we went at things a little backward. She hasn't agreed to date me yet, but she is pregnant with my baby." I used the human word instead of pup to signal to my parents the situation. It was one they were becoming familiar with because Audrey and Marina hadn't known about shifters when their mates had found them. They'd learned in time, and that was what I was asking for now. "Becky, if my mom ever lets you go, this is my dad, Tom."

"Nice to meet you." Becky extricated herself from my mom's embrace and shook my dad's hand. Little did she know, while he wasn't a hugger, he'd cover her hand with the other and refuse to let go.

"Becky," my dad said. His smile had spread to a big grin, and he was as shocked as Mom. We'd completely surprised them... and over lunch. "Not sure what to say in this situation other than we're both so pleased to know you. Sounds like you're not ready for a *welcome to the family*, but that's how we feel, just the same."

Because my parents would never break pack law and discuss our nature with a human who wasn't aware of our existence, I was sure I could trust them not to say anything to Becky before I'd had the chance.

And fuck! I sure as hell didn't know when that would be. If she couldn't even contemplate dating me yet, she wasn't going to easily wrap her mind around the concept of being mated for life. Especially considering I'd done it without her consent. She'd just thought I'd been a little wild in bed. Nothing more.

"Your parents must be excited," Dad said.

Becky offered him a small smile. "We're not close, actually. I haven't spoken to them in a few years. They won't be involved."

Mom's face fell, and Dad was silent. Shifters were all about family. Blood or chosen. We took care of each other. Becky's words made me want to track the couple down and bash their heads together for making her think she was an accident. Between her parents and Todd then me not being around—until now—during her pregnancy, she'd probably felt *very* alone. That ended now. I was sure my parents would see to that as much as me.

"Well, we're going to be involved. Too involved," Dad said, and Mom nodded.

Exactly. This was what families did. They got in the way. I *was* thankful that they were showing her that while getting pregnant had been an accident, our child wasn't one. It—she—was *very* wanted.

Becky pasted on a smile. "You have a lovely home, and it... it smells really good in here."

I laughed, letting her change the subject. "She's hungry, so let's put some food in front of her before you blast us with questions."

I was lucky, and I knew it. Not everyone had parents as kind and open-hearted as Rand and I did. They were a large part of what made our community —our pack—what it was. Rob had been sixteen when he'd become alpha, and Dad had really helped him in those early years. His advice was solid and respected.

Rand and his best friend, Nash, pushed through the front door. "We heard there was lasagna," he explained, gaze flicking over Becky with curiosity. "We couldn't turn that down."

My parents looked at me.

I wrapped an arm around Becky which said plenty in itself. "My brother Rand's the dark haired one, and Nash is the other."

They took off their hats and nodded.

"This is Becky and—"

Rand took a deep breath, eyes widening. "She's your m—"

"She's our lunch guest," Mom cut in, saving Rand from sticking his foot in his mouth. "Don't scare her off before she even takes off her coat."

Realizing she was right, I helped Becky get out of her jacket and tossed it at Rand. "Hang it up, runt. This is the woman who's making you an uncle."

He was far from little. In fact, he was taller and heavier than I was. But he was four years younger and had been small until he hit thirteen. Then, as my mom said, he grew overnight.

He held the coat in his hand as he opened his mouth in an exaggerated "O" and swung a *can you believe it* gaze at Nash. "No shit."

"Language, Rand," Mom scolded then reached out a hand to Becky. "Come into the kitchen and sit down. We'll try not to overwhelm you. We're so excited."

I held a chair out for Becky, and she slid into it, her stomach growling again. I sat beside her, my hand protectively on the back of her chair.

"How did you two meet?" Dad asked as Mom used a spatula to place a slice of lasagna on a plate then passed it to Becky.

She thanked Mom then looked up at me. "At Audrey's bachelorette party."

Mom stopped plating the next piece. "You're friends with Audrey?"

"We work together at the hospital. I'm a nurse."

"You'll move into a cabin up here like Audrey and Boyd or stay in town? Oh, you two can live in the rental." Mom glanced at Dad, who nodded.

"We're taking things slow," I said.

Nash hadn't said a word until now, but he snorted then tried to hide it by taking a sip of water.

"You've been gone for… work for some months," Dad said, taking his lasagna-filled plate and setting it before him.

"I know you work with the horses. Audrey told me. That takes you out of town?" Becky asked.

So many fucking secrets. No one at the table knew I was a council enforcer, so I had to give my usual lie, which came to me really fucking easily by now. "I visit other ranches working with them on their horse programs. Breeding. Things like that."

She blushed, and I got hard beneath the table at the virile thought that I'd bred her. Mom handed me my plate. Becky waited until everyone was served, her hands in her lap.

"Eat, dear," Mom said, picking up her fork and digging in. Only then did Becky begin.

"This is so good," Becky said after she swallowed her first bite then wiped her mouth with a napkin.

"Thank you. All my boys say it's their favorite."

"I can see why. And my stomach seems to like it."

"Weird cravings?" Mom asked.

"Avocados. Cocktail wieners."

"I love pigs and blankets. Remember, Ma, you used to make those all the time. With mustard," Rand added, staring off into space as he reminisced about his time with miniature hot dogs.

"If Becky likes them, I'll make them for her. You?" she shrugged at Rand then gave him a wink. "Only if you give me a grandbaby."

"We've got ultrasound pictures," Becky offered. "Of the baby. If you—"

"Of course, we do," Dad said, setting his hand on hers again.

Becky smiled. "It's in my purse."

As she started to stand, I did as well. "I'll get it."

She shook her head. "No, it's fine. I'll get it, and if it's all right, may I use the bathroom?"

"The first door down the hall," Mom said.

She left the room, and everyone remained still waiting to hear the bathroom door close.

"You claimed her," Dad said.

"She doesn't know you're a shifter," Mom added.

"She's having your baby?" Rand asked.

"Holy shit, dude," Nash whispered.

If it was a shifter in the bathroom, we wouldn't even be able to talk without being overheard, but Becky wouldn't be able to hear our conversation.

What they hadn't said, because they didn't know, was that I was also an enforcer. It made things even more fucked up.

"When we first met, I had no idea she was my mate. My nose was broken. I won't share more—"

"Thank you," Mom cut in, then pursed her lips. I was thirty-four years old. She knew I wasn't a virgin, but that didn't mean she wanted details.

"—but I've been out of town for Rob. I had no idea about her or the baby until I ran into her at the grocery store the other day. Caught her scent."

"Only *you* wouldn't know a female was your

mate." Rand reached over and punched me on the arm and rolled his eyes.

"Wait until you find your mate and see what happens. You're going to have a story of your own to share."

Rand looked to Nash, who shrugged and shoveled a piece of lasagna into his mouth.

"How did you claim her without her knowing?" Nash asked.

I stared at him, then glanced at Mom, whose eyes narrowed at Nash.

"Yeah, never mind," he added.

"You need to tell her," Dad advised.

I sighed because it wasn't as simple as he thought. "I will. There's a lot to adjust to here. I'm trying not to completely freak her out."

The bathroom door opened, and there wasn't time to tell them about her problems with her ex or even the fact that she was still married. My parents wouldn't care. They didn't have a legal human wedding and had never expected me or Rand to have one. Todd was her ex and in the past. That was all that mattered to them. But they wouldn't be happy about the shit he was pulling, and I was sure they'd pull Selena in to help if I hadn't already.

I'd claimed Becky. She was mine. That's what

they learned when they picked up my scent on her. Nothing else mattered. She was family now.

She came back into the room holding the strip of pictures. "I guess we could call this our gender reveal party." She sat down and passed the ultrasound to my mom, who put her fingers over her lips as she stared at the black and white blobs.

My dad blinked at me. "I have no idea what that means."

I shrugged, pointing at the paper in Mom's hand. "Me neither. But it's a girl."

"Ohhhhh!" Mom hugged the ultrasound to her chest. "I can't believe it." A film of tears filled her eyes.

Becky took my hand beneath the table, and I gave it a squeeze. We had shit to figure out, but everything was going to be fine.

Dad swallowed hard then looked over at Mom fondly. "You finally get your girl, Janny."

Rand punched me in the arm again. "A girl who's going to wrap you around her little finger? You're fucked, dude."

"Language, Rand," my mom admonished, but this time there was a smile in her voice.

13

Becky

"Oh my God, aren't you beautiful?" I dropped to my knees in the warm stable in front of the baby foal, just three days old. I was sure it was the hormones—or maybe just coming from the warmth of Clint's parents' kitchen and all their joy over our baby—but tears filled my eyes at the sweetness in front of me.

The tiny horse stood on spindly legs, his black coat sleek. He had a white star-shaped marking on his nose, just like his gorgeous mama, Angelwing. She stood behind him and chuffed softly, proud to show her little black beauty off to us.

I thought of Clint's parents, of how they were proud of him, even though he'd gotten a stranger pregnant. They'd embraced me with open arms. Literally. When my parents had found out I was leaving Todd, they'd been stunned. I'd found a *doctor*, and I should be thankful for the marriage I had.

As if. When I'd told my mother the list of reasons, like Todd hitting me, she'd asked what I'd done to make him mad.

They'd put their foot down, ashamed to have a divorced daughter, and said if I didn't stay in my marriage, they'd cast me out. As if they were the example of a perfect marriage themselves.

Cast me out were the actual words they'd used.

Janet and Tom wouldn't do that to their kids, no matter what they'd done. They didn't say that, but I knew. They were a family. A real family, and it had felt special to be included.

Extra special, it seemed, when Janet had pulled out the big guns for dessert, brownies with homemade hot fudge. Rand had whined and asked why I got the hot fudge when he never did.

We'd all laughed at his fake pout, and Janet had told him if he made her a grandbaby, then she'd make him hot fudge.

We stayed an hour after that before Clint drove

me down the hill to show me where he worked. And this gorgeous four-legged baby.

"Do you want to name him?" Clint asked. He stood beside me, a hand in his jeans pocket.

I glanced up at him. I'd been to the ranch before but never in the stable. This was where Clint spent his time. I delivered human babies, and he delivered foals. We had more in common than I thought.

I set my hand on my chest. "Me? Is that allowed?"

Clint chuckled, tipped his hat back. "Sure, it's allowed. This is Rob's ranch, but the horse breeding project is mine." He crouched beside me and rubbed the little foal's forehead.

"So his mama is Angelwing," I said thoughtfully, considering. I reached out to stroke the star on his forehead, too. "Maybe he should be Starshine."

"Starshine." Clint stroked the foal's neck. "What do you think of that, little fella?"

The sweet baby leaned forward and nuzzled my neck. I giggled at the softness.

"I think that means he likes it."

The sweet scent of hay and the tang of animals filled the air, but it was cozy in here. Warm and safe. "What will you do with him when he grows up? Sell him? Or breed him?" I was suddenly overcome by the desire to beg to keep the animal, even though I'd only ridden a horse twice in my life. I might have grown up about fifty miles from here, but I wasn't a true cowgirl, not like I would have been if I'd grown up here on Wolf Ranch. Visions of Clint lifting our daughter onto Starshine's back filled my mind. *She'd* be a cowgirl. He'd see to it. A rush of longing for just that filled me, but they were only foolish thoughts.

I barely knew Clint. And while yes, he seemed like a stand-up guy and our attraction was off the charts, that didn't mean we had a happily ever after in our future. I couldn't let myself believe that, not even with a baby between us. I'd tried to talk myself into that scenario with Todd for years. I'd pretended he would change or could become the perfect father to a family. I'd tried to force my fate to happen for me, and it hadn't gotten me anywhere except in a pile of dog poop.

So, no. I wasn't going to sign on with the next guy who came along, even if he was a mountain of handsome goodness who also happened to father my unborn child. I just didn't believe in that happily ever after thing anymore. Not for me.

Maybe for others, like Audrey had with Boyd. They were having a baby, too. Sure, she'd gotten pregnant before getting married, but they'd known each other, fallen in love.

I wasn't doing that with Clint... was I?

"I don't know yet," he commented, breaking me from my thoughts. "I might keep him for breeding. Depends on how big he ends up growing. But his sire was almost seventeen hands, so he could be a big one." Clint pinned me with a look. "Why? You want him?"

My lips parted in surprise. Was it really that easy? My face grew warm. "Offering a Montana girl a pony? Yes. God, yes, but that's stupid. I don't know anything about horses. I'm sure it's my hormones, but I feel like I'm in love with this little guy already."

I rubbed his little nose some more.

Clint shook his head. "No, that happens. Horses seem to pick their person just like wolves pick their life mate."

Something about his words made goosebumps race across my arms and a wing flap in my belly. "What do you know about wolves?" I asked carefully.

Clint's gaze locked onto mine. "Quite a bit, actually." He stood and swept me into his arms, as was becoming his habit.

"Clint!" I cried as he carried me to a stack of hay bales and set me down, caging my waist with his large hands. *Oh my.*

"Wolves are the most loyal species in the animal

kingdom. Did you know that?" He pushed me to my back and crawled over me, his lips finding my neck beneath the collar of my coat.

"What are you doing?" I breathed although I had a pretty good idea.

He licked a line up my neck. "It's been hours since I've had my hands on you."

"We're in the stables. Anyone can walk in." I stared up at the wooden rafters as he kept kissing me, clearly not concerned.

"I'll hear them." He cupped my sex, grinding his palm down over my clit. "The grey wolf, in particular, is eternally loyal to his mate, but the entire pack forms life bonds with each other. Only the alpha male and female will reproduce."

I moaned at the pleasure he was able to pull from me so quickly. In the Wolf stables. God, I would melt for him anywhere. Cody's storage room. Here. I was a slut for his attention. I was close to coming, and we were wearing all our clothes. What could he do if he got me naked? Or half naked? Or… just sliding my panties to the side. Oh yeah, pregnant. I moaned when he kissed a spot behind my ear and rubbed my clit just right. Damn hormones.

"Y-you must consider yourself an expert on breeding," I teased, writhing beneath him.

He bit my nipple through my bra and sweater. When he lifted his head, his grin was downright wicked. "Oh, sugar. You have no idea."

I gulped. "Maybe I do since, you know, I'm knocked up."

He unbuttoned my jeans—which I wasn't going to be able to wear much longer—and dragged the zipper down as he gave me a wink. "Did you know male wolves lick a female's genitals to test her readiness?" He brought his face between my legs and bit through the fabric. I sensed the heat of his mouth, even through my jeans. When he moved to tug them and my panties down, I lifted my butt to help. As if I was going to stop him. "Same as us, only they're tasting her hormones."

Slowly, he took off his cowboy hat and set it on the bale beside me, the entire time keeping his eyes focused on mine. Then he watched me as his tongue slid along my slit.

"Oh my God," I moaned, my hips lifting into him.

"I'm just tasting your delicious nectar."

Nectar? Whatever, as long as he didn't stop. I grabbed his head, pulling his mouth into my dripping core. "Clint," I moaned, my chin arcing toward the ceiling with pleasure. "I-I've been so horny with this pregnancy. I thought for sure it meant I was having a boy."

Clint made his tongue stiff and penetrated me with it. "I think it means you got pregnant with the right guy," he said smugly before he returned to treating me to heaven with his tongue. I made a keening sound. My breasts had grown heavy, nipples tight and stiff inside my bra.

"Clint," I moaned again as he found his way back to my clit. He teased the stiff bud with his tongue then affixed his lips over it and sucked.

I clapped a hand over my mouth to hold in my scream. It felt so good. I didn't want it to stop, and yet I was desperate for the finish at the same time. "I can't—I can't—" I panted.

Clint paused, damn him and looked up at me from between my shamelessly parted thighs. "You can't what?"

"Please don't stop," I gasped. "Oh, please, I'm so close."

He chuckled, his hot breath bathing my flesh. "I know what you need," he claimed, the cocky bastard. And he was right. He knew exactly what I needed.

"Why is it like this with you? It's... intense. I swear, I've never felt like this before."

He growled. Actually growled then softened it

with a melty look. "Sugar." Then he got to work, sucking hard on my clit as he inserted two fingers in my channel, curling them up to hit my g-spot. As an Ob/Gyn nurse, I knew the workings of the female anatomy very well. But it seemed Clint's knowledge blew mine to bits because when he found my back pucker with his thumb, I left the stratosphere orgasming so hard. My belly jumped, inner walls sucked on his fingers, anus pulled in and the stable spun in circles as I turned inside out.

It was possible my scream had scared Starshine. The intensity of it sure scared me. I'd never had anyone touch my ass before during sex. Well, ever. I was going to have to change my thoughts about that because holy hell, that had pushed me over the edge.

I didn't know how much time passed before my vision cleared and I became aware of my surroundings again. The stable. My panting breath. Clint's satisfied smirk as he slid his fingers out and licked them, one after the other as if he was getting the last bits of a tasty treat. His mouth and chin were glistening. Oh my god, I was all over him. I should have been mortified, but I was too well pleasured to give a shit. My horniness was soothed, for the moment.

"I'm gonna be hard all fucking evening thinking

about that." He reached down and adjusted himself. I looked, saw how big he was pressed against his zipper. He was a big cowboy... all over.

"Sorry," I said automatically, biting my lip.

He shook his head. "Don't you dare apologize. You have needs, sugar, and it's my job to take care of them."

"I'm not usually this... horny."

He grinned. "You won't hear me complaining. Watching you come is a fucking *gift*." He pulled my jeans back up and zipped and buttoned me in them, making me feel cherished as hell. Making me think what a great dad he would make. "I'll take care of you again when we get in bed later, naked."

His phone rang, and he pulled it from his coat pocket. "It's Rob, I need to take this, okay?" He held up a finger and paced away. "Yeah. Actually, I'm in the stable with Becky. Yes, Audrey's friend. Yes. Yes. Okay." He glanced over at me. "That should work. Hang on." He pulled the phone from his ear and looked at me. "Audrey and Marina are at the main house with Willow, Rob's wife, for a ladies' happy hour if you want to join them. I need to stop in and talk to Rob for a bit. Would that work, sugar?"

Wow. A man who asked what I wanted to do before making plans. It shouldn't seem novel, but it was. Clint was considerate. And yes, girl time sounded fabulous. Audrey was my BFF, and I knew Marina, but hadn't met Willow yet. If she could tame moody Rob, then I knew I was going to like her.

"That sounds fun." I hopped down from the hay bale.

Clint stepped close and pulled a piece of straw from my hair. "I like seeing you all mussed and know I got you that way. I'm not sharing it with others though." He leaned down, kissed my forehead. "You're all mine."

14

Clint

"What's up?" I followed Rob into his office, shutting out the laughter and chatter of the women in the great room.

While Audrey, Marina and Willow were surprised to see Becky with me, they'd embraced her with open arms, literally, then shooed me and Rob out to catch up. Becky seemed happy, so it was easy for me to leave her. I was totally whipped since she was just down the fucking hall. But, I was here at my alpha's request, and now I had to focus on whatever he had to say.

"You tell me." Rob leaned a hip against his desk

and crossed his arms over his chest. "You've claimed her."

"I have."

"You've been back in town, what, four days? You move fast."

"As if you're one to talk." I tapped my finger on my chin. "If I remember correctly, you got one whiff of Willow and slammed a door in my face."

The corner of Rob's mouth turned up, which for him, was a wide grin.

"She's pregnant," I said.

A dark brow went up, his only sign of surprise. "Four days. You've been back four fucking days. How do you know she's—"

"Audrey's bachelorette party. The storage room at Cody's. Potent swimmers who got past a condom." I gave him the short and sweet version. We were best friends, but we didn't share details of our sex lives. No doubt he could scent Becky's arousal all over me from what I did to her in the stable. That was enough.

"You knew back then she was your mate and left to track down Jarod Jameson?" His voice rumbled with quiet anger. Mates didn't leave their females unprotected. Not for a day and especially not for months, like I had.

"If I'd known she was my mate, you think I wouldn't have told you? I'd have ensured you watched out for her. Had pack protection."

"How did you not know?"

"I got punched in the fucking nose by an asshole messing with Becky that night at Cody's. I couldn't start a bar fight, no matter how much I wanted to rip the guy's throat out. It was the middle of Audrey's party, and I know your rules."

He nodded once.

"My nose was broken. I couldn't scent her. I wanted her even when I didn't know she was mine."

Even Rob couldn't say that.

He sighed. "I'm guessing you're going to tell me you're done, that an enforcer spot just opened up."

"Yeah."

He frowned. "Unfortunately, it might not be that easy." Going around the desk, he settled into his chair, dropped his head back as if he had shit to deal with, and it was exhausting.

I waited, stifling the low growl I wanted to issue at any potential threat to my mate. Me remaining council enforcer would definitely be a threat, even if the only issue was being gone for long stretches. But that wasn't the only problem. It was a dangerous job, while I was gone and once I got home. If the wrong shifters found out my identity, everyone I loved could be in danger.

"Word out of the Madison Range pack—"

"Is Sal Brown still causing you trouble?" I asked.

He waved his hand through the air. "Not him, but it turns out Jarod Jameson was his nephew."

A spike of cold stabbed at the base of my head. I set my hat on the corner of his desk and ran a hand across the back of my neck, trying to rub out the feeling. "Fuck."

"I guess the kid didn't grow up in the same pack. Sal's sister mated someone in the Clear Lake pack. She settled there and raised the nephew. While I guess they didn't really keep in touch and Sal never even met Jameson, he's got a beef with him being taken out."

"Of course, he fucking does," I grumbled. "That man's nothing but a—"

Rob held up his hand. "I know what he is. Word is, his son, Donald, Jarod's cousin, is getting up in the council members' asses trying to sniff out the identity of the enforcer who finished Jameson."

I dropped into a chair, sighed. "Fucking hell. Don't they have any clue that my actions are *ordered* by the council? Jameson was a low-life drug addict. He tore the throats out of convenience store workers. He had to be taken out before more died and before humans caught on the murders were done by a shifter."

"I know, but Donald still wants revenge. They're saying the council should have let the family handle it because the kid had a drug problem. You know, that *it wasn't his fault, it was the drugs* and all that bullshit."

"Well, I agree he had a problem. They should've tracked him down and helped him before the council declared his life forfeit. Wasn't my goddamn decision," I snapped. "An eye for an eye is shifter law in a nutshell. I don't make the rules." When Rob didn't reply because he fucking knew that, too, I continued. "I got a slice in my side from Jarod that's taking it's fucking time to heal."

He frowned. "Silver?"

I nodded, setting my hand on my side. "It's almost gone, but it's been days. I'll never take shifter healing for granted again." It was a good thing Becky had wanted it dark the other night. She'd missed the wound, which would have been hard to explain. The next time I got her in bed, it would barely be a pink mark. Thank fuck.

"I don't want a repeat of that shit with his cousin."

"I think he's not going to let this go."

I shrugged. "Fine, Donald has something to do to keep his thumb out of his ass all winter. He'll find nothing. The identities of enforcers are locked tight. You're the only non-council member who knows I'm one of them."

Rob met my gaze. His expression was normally serious, but it was doubly so now. "I sure as fuck hope so. I told the council to pay a visit to the family to try to calm things down, but they're too high and mighty to do it. I'd do it myself, but it would show my hand. I don't need them knowing we have an interest."

I stilled, my heart even skipping a beat. Rob's concern that I'd be found instilled chaos in my world. No one found an enforcer. Not unless someone on the council talked. My identity was supposed to be secret even from my own goddamn family. If the council called in an enforcer to take action, the task was sanctioned. There were no repercussions from the outcome on the enforcer. It was also pack law. Everyone knew that, even Sal and Donald.

"Well, I didn't drop my fucking ID on the ground when I finished the asshole. I'm not that bad at my job."

"No, but I hear they're asking around. Trying to figure out which enforcer's signature is the bullet behind the left ear."

"Fuck." I popped to my feet. *"Becky."* I stared at Rob in horror. His lips tightened, evidence of his own concern. "Holy fuck. I've brought shit right to her. This... this is the exact reason I tried to stay away from her even after I realized she was mine."

Rob rasped a hand over his jaw. "With a pup on the way?"

"Before I knew about the pup. She's married and—"

"Excuse me?" Rob leaned forward.

It was my turn to frown, rub my eyes. I explained the situation with her ex and what I'd learned from the data-digger's online search.

"You get Selena involved, too?"

"Yesterday. We're staying at my parents' place in town. The ex won't find her there."

"Good. Explain to me how you're going to stay away from her to protect her from enforcer shit when she's got an ex fucking with her."

I gave him a dark stare. "Fuck you."

He stood, came around the desk. "Glad to see it's my best friend's turn to be mauled by Fate and a female."

"Again, fuck you," I grumbled.

He leaned against the side of his desk. "Selena can help with her ex."

He lifted his head, listened. Knew he was taking a moment to check on the ladies. With my wolf hearing, I picked up their laughter. They were fine, and that soothed my wolf. Now that I had a mate to protect, I could see how hard it was for Rob to always be listening and watching, protecting not just Willow but the entire pack. Everyone in the house fell under his rule and protection.

It made me thankful to only be an enforcer, a job I could quit. Rob had his role for life.

"As for Donald Brown, let's talk about what we're going to do. I'll call the council and tell them you have a mate now, and there's more at stake than just a threat to an enforcer. This guy might show up on pack land. We need a plan."

I nodded and we got to work coming up with one.

15

Becky

"So... you and Clint?" Audrey prodded, with a waggle of her eyebrows and a grin. "Girlfriend, you've been keeping secrets."

We sat in the great room in the big comfy couches that shaped a U and faced the massive river rock fireplace. Beside it, built into the wall, was a TV with the first *Twilight* movie playing. Delicious hors d'oeuvres Marina had baked were on the coffee table in front of us. Marina and Willow had wine, Audrey lemon tea. When the ladies said they had happy hour together like this at least once a week, I experienced a pang of jealousy. I wanted to be part of their tribe, too. Which I guessed I could be, if Clint and I became a fixture.

They were all comfortable in leggings, soft sweaters and thick socks. Audrey had a cozy blanket tucked around her.

The three of them lived on the ranch—Audrey up in the hills in a cute cabin, Marina and Colton finally settling into one of their own as well, and Willow here in the family house—so it was easy for them to do so. In fact, there wasn't much else to do out here, especially in the winter.

I flushed at Audrey's words, only because she knew about my divorce efforts. Namely, the fact that it wasn't finalized, and I was getting it on with Clint. I still had that religious shame ingrained in me by my parents. Marriage was a sacrament. One that shouldn't be broken even if it sucked.

Even if the guy broke you. And your car tire. And emptied your bank account. And...

"It's nothing serious," I replied, finally. It wasn't a total lie. I'd told Clint I couldn't enter into a relationship with him. He knew where I stood. Of course, the fact that we were having a child together might be considered serious to some. Some might also think the fact that we'd slept together the night before... sex *and* actual sleeping, plus what he'd just done to me in the stable, constituted us being together.

Hell, I'd had lunch with his parents. *That* was a big deal.

Shit.

Willow tucked her hair behind her ear and said, "It smells serious to me." Her nostrils flared like she was actually smelling something.

"Smells?" I raised my eyebrows at the strange turn of phrase.

She got busy reaching for the bottle of wine, kept her eyes focused on the task. "I just mean, we haven't seen Clint with any woman, ever. So, if he's bringing you here to look at newborn foals, it means something."

Warmth kindled in my chest. I shouldn't be so happy to hear he never brought women around, but I was. He wasn't a monk. I knew he'd been with women before me. A gorgeous cowboy like him, a virgin at thirty-four? As if.

"We had lunch with his parents. And brother. And Nash," I added. All three of them stared as if I'd said I'd eaten with the Queen. "What?"

"And it's not serious?" Willow asked. "Are you sure because while I haven't known Clint all that long, no guy takes a woman to meet his parents unless it's serious. Especially around here. You sure you don't want some wine?" She held up the bottle of chardonnay.

"No, no. I'll stick with water." I pointed to the glass Marina had gotten me when I'd first arrived, a thin slice of lemon floating on the top.

All three eyed me with curiosity. I may or may not have been the one who usually led the party when it came to imbibing a few. What could I say? I'd always had a lot of steam to let off after getting out from Todd's clutches. Audrey's bachelorette party had been the perfect example. I'd organized it with Marina, and while a limo had been on the schedule, me having sex with Clint in the storage room had not.

"Okay, I'm pregnant, too!" I blurted because Audrey was also having a baby—just a few weeks ahead of me.

"Oh my God!" Audrey sang, throwing her arms wide and giving me a hug as she leaned across the couch. "Wait… is it Clint's?"

I nodded, blushing. "Your bachelorette party. We kind of hooked up."

"That was months ago!" Audrey said. I recognized her doctor's gaze as she looked me over.

"I can't believe you didn't tell me. I am an Ob/Gyn," she muttered the last as if she was put out.

"I'm seeing Dr. Seymour. I didn't come to you because there's no way I could have my bestie staring at my lady parts with my feet up in stirrups."

She rolled her eyes then nodded. "Yeah, that makes sense."

"I didn't tell anyone because, you know—my life is a mess right now," I added. I looked to Marina and Willow and realized they knew nothing about my fiasco with Todd. I gave them the short version of how Todd had behaved in the marriage and my reason for leaving.

"Asshole," Marina muttered, grabbing a stuffed mushroom and popping it in her mouth.

"That's what I've been dealing with. Besides, twenty percent of first pregnancies end in miscarriage. I didn't see the point in, well, facing it, until I was sure it would stick."

"Clint didn't know?" Marina asked, whispering. Her excitement was palpable—she practically bubbled over with enthusiasm, which made me feel much better about my deceit.

I shook my head. "Not at first. The first time I saw him since your party was the other day. I puked on his shoes at the grocery store." I tossed out a rueful smile as they gasped. "I didn't tell him then. The next night, actually. Well, I didn't tell him. He figured it out." I flushed, remembering our lovemaking that night. How he'd recognized the changes in my body. How he'd made me feel beautiful despite them.

They whooped and laughed, knowing what I meant.

"So you're not taking the relationship seriously, but I'm guessing Clint is?" Audrey asked, eyeing me carefully.

Willow and Marina watched me, too, hanging for my answer. I got the feeling they knew something I didn't. Something I should know—about Clint.

"I did meet his parents, but that's not the reason for your question. What makes you ask?"

Marina jumped up and arranged some more cheese popovers onto a plate. Willow refilled Marina's glass then went to a little mini-fridge in the corner for another bottle.

"Why do I feel like you guys know something I don't?"

"Oh, we know these ranch boys, that's all," Audrey said quickly. "I'm pretty sure Clint's just like the Wolf brothers—fiercely protective and completely loyal. You've seen them. I mean, you remember how Colton and Boyd crashed the bachelorette party. I guess Clint did too now that I think about it. Don't worry, the guy's not going to shirk his responsibility when it comes to a baby."

Responsibility.

I didn't like that word. It was one of the reasons I hadn't told Clint in the first place. I didn't want to get tangled in a relationship just because we were having a kid together. I wasn't one of those people who believed having a kid out of wedlock was a sin, even though my parents did. I believed marrying the wrong person was a sin.

One I'd been paying for… for years.

They were all watching me again, so I offered them a fake smile then owned up. "I'm sure the baby will appreciate that, but I'm not jumping into a relationship just because a condom didn't work. You know what I mean?"

Marina's eyes widened slightly, like she was taken aback.

"I don't want to just be Clint's responsibility. I want to be… more."

Audrey jumped to my rescue. "Of course, you do. I know you're still in the middle of a tricky divorce." She covered my hand with hers. "I'm sure this seems like terrible timing."

My bank account had been wiped out, and I wasn't exactly sure how I was going to pay the rent this month. Sure, I'd have the money with my next paycheck, which I'd have to get cashed then give the landlord money in an envelope to ensure Todd didn't get his mean fingers on it. I frowned at how much of a pain that would be. Yet I had no extra money. I literally had nothing to my name. Wasn't that fucking depressing?

I nodded at Audrey, a lump in my throat forming.

"I hope you don't feel like Clint is pressuring you. These ranch guys come on strong—we can all attest to that."

Marina and Willow nodded.

I released a watery laugh. "He definitely comes on strong. I told you about why I'm divorcing my ex, but not the latest with him. Todd is causing all kinds of trouble right now. Clint caught him looking in my bedroom window, so Clint pretty much made me pack a bag and move in with him. He said it won't hurt us to get to know each other while he's protecting me."

The women all looked concerned. "Todd was looking in your window?" Audrey asked. "That's creepy. I'm so glad Clint was there to help."

"Yeah, and that was right after Todd drained my

bank account and slashed my tire. God, I just wish he'd meet someone else and get over me. Or drop dead," I added.

Marina put another cheese puff on my plate, as if feeding me would solve my problems. "Well, I think Clint's right. I'm glad you have him to protect you," she said.

"Me, too," Audrey concurred.

Willow also nodded gravely. "Do you have a gun? I could teach you to shoot."

I remembered Audrey telling me she was former D.E.A. and smiled. She'd pretended to be the new next-door neighbor to investigate a drug runner who'd bought the adjacent property. I didn't know where the neighbor was now. Willow had only said she still hadn't moved to the ranch.

"No, I'm not a fan of guns. But thanks." I gobbled down the cheese puff and half the glass of water. Even after eating two helpings of lasagna, I was hungry. Marina's snacks were so good, even without any little hot dogs. "Anyway, the bottom line is that my life's a freaking mess. Clint and I are going to stay in the getting-to-know-you phase until it's not. End of story."

Willow nodded, watching me thoughtfully.

"Right. That makes sense. Hopefully Clint can dial it back." Her gaze tracked to my neck.

I found myself reaching up to cover the place he'd bitten me even though I didn't think it showed under my shirt. Now all three of them stared at the spot. I quickly put my hand down and grabbed a stuffed mushroom from the loaded plate.

"Let me ask you this." Marina leaned forward on her forearms. "If circumstances were different—if the divorce was in the past and there was no pregnancy—would you be interested in Clint?"

I thought of every interaction I'd had with the hot horse wrangler—which granted, hadn't been that many—and how they'd all left me aglow. He'd been attentive, hot, sexy, dominant. His kindness showed through in the way he handled me. The way he handled that sweet foal. Unlike Todd, he seemed humble—he didn't boast or show off. Like how he didn't get upset about having his nose broken at the bar. It hadn't been about him proving anything, it had been about me. Protecting me.

Then there were the times he wasn't overly gentlemanly. When he laid me over a hay bale, parted my thighs and ate me out until I screamed his name. Or fucked me rough and wild up against a storage room wall, completely lost to the pleasure he got from me and my body.

My pussy clenched at the idea of more of both the hot cowboy and dirty talker. "Definitely," I answered. "I would definitely want to explore things with Clint."

"Well, let's explore, sugar," Clint said from the doorway, and I blushed to my roots.

I narrowed my eyes and pointed at Marina. "You knew he was there."

She looked sheepish but not sorry.

I turned, balled up a napkin and tossed it at him. "You weren't supposed to be listening!"

He shook his head even though he was grinning. "I didn't hear a thing. Just something about exploring." He waggled his eyebrows like I'd been talking about sex. I was glad he couldn't read my thoughts. "I'm down for anything, so long as it involves you." He held out his hand, like I was a lady in Regency times who required a man's assistance to stand.

These were the little things he did that made me feel like a queen. Maybe I could explore things with him. A relationship. A *real* one. Maybe this one time, life wouldn't fuck me over.

"Willow, thanks for feeding my girl, but we've got

to get back to town. She works in the morning, so she's got to get to bed early."

Audrey laughed. "Yeah, Boyd says the same thing, but it never means to sleep!"

Based on what Clint promised in the barn, I didn't think it meant to sleep either.

16

Clint

THE NEXT DAY, I knelt next to Starshine to check on him, and my mind flooded with images of Becky. No way I could ever get rid of this foal now. He would forever remind me of my mate. I'd worked hard all morning mucking out the stalls and riding four of the horses, but my mind had never left her.

She was scheduled to work today. While I wished she'd have called in sick, I'd agreed the hospital was safe enough after she'd explained to me that the Labor and Delivery and Mom/Baby areas were kept on lock-down. The security there was tight, and no one could get on the floor without proper ID. Even her ex, or so she promised me. She knew what he could do more than me, and I trusted her that she was thinking of her safety when I'd dropped her off for her shift.

But when Rob came into the stable, and I caught the urgency in the way he said my name, my wolf took notice.

"Audrey called," he told me. "She wanted to get a message to you. Sheriff Duncan went to the hospital and picked up Becky for questioning."

"What?" I barked. My chest puffed and my hands clenched into fists. My wolf howled in anger.

Rob was calm, as usual. "He had a deputy with him. While she wasn't under arrest, they read her her Miranda rights and took her to the station."

The stable spun. I may have partially shifted because my vision sharpened like I was on a hunt. The growl that filled the stable made the horses whinny with fear. I reached out, set my hand on a hay bale. I gripped it in my fingers, lifted it with one hand and tossed it across the stable.

"For what?" I demanded, my breath coming out in ragged pants. I couldn't lose my shit here. My mate was in fucking jail, and she needed me.

He didn't step closer, just gave me room to lose my shit.

"Her ex was found murdered in her place last night."

I was already moving, jogging out of the stable to my truck assuming he'd follow. "What? Murdered? *In* her house? What the fuck was he doing there, and how did he get inside?"

"I don't know that. I only know what Audrey told me," he called from behind me.

"Tell her I'm on my way."

"Hold up, Clint," Rob barked. He must've used alpha command because that was the only thing that would've stopped my feet, and they skidded to a halt. I stood in the packed dirt area in front of the stable. My truck was a hundred feet away in front of the bunkhouse. I could get in it, get to town and be with my mate within thirty minutes. Except my alpha commanded me to wait.

"Listen to me," he said. "The guy *had his throat ripped out.*"

I spun around to face him. "What the fuck? Who rips—oh shit."

"This was a message." He came up to me, set his hands on his hips. "I think Donald found you. Scented you. Followed you to Becky's. Knows she's yours."

My eyes widened at what he was saying.

No.

No!

I opened my mouth to bellow, but Rob shot out more of that alpha command. "Keep your damn head."

"It's my fault. My mate *and unborn child* are in jail because of me. This was why I tried to keep my distance. I knew all along I was nothing but trouble for her."

I spun around, faced my truck and kicked a huge dent in the side panel. Then I ripped off the side view mirror, hurled it across the parking area.

He clapped a heavy hand on my shoulder, grounding me. Stopping me. "You need to call Selena to meet you at the jail. Becky needs a lawyer who knows human law and understands what the fuck really happened."

I was seething, but his words penetrated. They made sense. Selena could deal with the sheriff and the questioning. Becky had been with me for over twenty-four hours when I dropped her off at the hospital. I had no idea when Todd had been killed, but it had to have been in that window since he'd gone into her house after he'd been released from custody. That meant Becky wasn't a suspect, only the dead guy's widow. Being a shifter, Selena would recognize the cause of death and know it was shifter related and put it together.

Selena'd have Becky out fast, but that didn't make it any better knowing she was there alone right now. And that wouldn't solve the issue with Donald.

"Get your mate out of there and somewhere you can protect her. I'll update the council. They'll want to know about this." He didn't release his grip on my shoulder. "Your wolf is still showing," he said.

My eyes must've still been silver. I was growling, too. A low, menacing rumble meant to tell the world to back the fuck away from my mate.

Becky.

Fates, she must be so scared. So traumatized. Her ex, murdered in her own home.

And it was my fucking fault!

I brought this on her.

Fuck, fuck, fuck!

"I knew I should've stayed away from her, but I just couldn't help myself, could I?"

"Clint." Rob gave me an alpha growl, and my mind settled.

"What would you do if this was Willow?"

"You'd tell me the exact same thing," he countered. "Pull it together, man. Your mate needs you to have a clear head."

I nodded. Yes. He was right. I sucked in a deep breath through my nostrils and blew it out. "I'm good," I promised.

He studied me. "Are you? Because I'm not letting you go to the station if you're gonna go silver there."

I swallowed. "No, I'm good. I'm good. Let me go."

Rob released his hold on me. "Keep it together."

"Yeah. I'm good," I chanted, opening the truck door. I wasn't going to kill anyone at the station. Even if I wanted to. I would save it all for Donald Brown. The guy who dared threaten my mate. The guy who entered her fucking house last night.

The guy who was going to die. Very soon. I wasn't a council enforcer now. I was a mate whose female was in danger.

I got on my phone as I drove into town. "Selena," I said in a tight voice when she answered. "The police have my mate. Her ex was murdered in her house."

"Where is she being held?"

"The Cooper Valley station."

"I'll meet you there. They aren't going to let you in, so don't kick up a fuss when you get there. Tell them her lawyer is on her way. Let me handle things."

I growled, not thrilled with what she said. "Fine.

There's something else. Something you need to know. Consider it client-attorney privilege."

"Oh Fates. Tell me you didn't kill him."

I gripped the steering wheel until it cracked. "I didn't. But it was a wolf shifter, for sure. His throat was torn out."

She sighed. "What else?"

"I'm a council enforcer. I think I brought this on Becky. Someone's out for revenge, and they're fucking with my mate to make me sweat."

"That's a problem. A very big problem. Because if I can get Becky released from there today—"

"You mean when," I snarled.

"I'll do my best. But when I do, you won't be able to leave town or go into hiding. She'll need to stay where the police can contact her. If she's a suspect in this murder case, she won't be allowed to leave town."

"Which means we'll be sitting ducks."

"Unfortunately, yes."

I roared my fury, stepping on the gas. Things couldn't be any more fucked up. And all I knew was that I had to get Becky into my arms. I had to know she was safe and provided for, or I was going to lose my ever-loving mind.

17

Becky

"Trash can," I croaked, hand over my mouth.

Sheriff Duncan shoved it toward me as I lurched from my chair to puke again.

I couldn't believe Todd was dead. Not just dead. Murdered. In my house!

They seemed to think I'd done it.

My body shook involuntarily, the nerves turning me into a rattling cage. I glanced down at my lavender scrubs. God, they'd come for me at work. I'd been late the other day and now this. No question

I'd lose my job, and I'd be getting a call from the nursing board.

"Are you all right?"

I turned my head and glared at the deputy who had a gun on his hip but probably wasn't old enough to buy himself a drink.

"So, you're saying you haven't been to your house at all in the past thirty-six hours?" Sheriff Duncan asked. The room was full of officers—the sheriff from Meade as well as probably every Cooper Valley deputy on duty. It wasn't as if murder ever happened in this small backwater town. Until now.

I blinked away tears, feeling alone. Scared. I had no idea what to do. Todd had harassed me while he was alive, and he was still messing with me when he was dead. I stood and hugged the trash can to my chest.

"I left right after you took Todd away the night before last," I explained, for the fourth time, wiping my mouth with the back of my hand. "Clint took me to his parents' place for lunch yesterday, and we stayed at Wolf Ranch until around seven. We stayed at Clint's parents' rental last night. Together."

Clint. *Clint.* I'd told him I couldn't have a relationship, and he'd seen why firsthand. Todd had destroyed my life, and I hadn't wanted to pull Clint into it. I'd *told* him! He'd see my words for what they were: the truth. There was no way he'd want to be with me after this. I wasn't worth his time and energy. He should have listened to me before taking me to Wolf Ranch, letting me get a glimpse of what a real family was like. To fall for not just Clint but his mom and dad, too. Then to hang with the girls last night and get a glimpse of what it would be like to be in a relationship with Clint—because being with Clint meant being with his family and friends, too. He had a lot of them. It had been hard to push him away the other day. Now?

Fuck, I'd fallen for him. Stupid.

"Why didn't you stay at your house?"

I took a deep breath, tried to swallow my tears and keep them and the dregs in my stomach, down. "Because Clint didn't want Todd to know where I was."

"So you were in danger from Todd? I've heard from witnesses it was the other way around."

"What?"

"You threatened him in the parking lot of Bishop's Mechanic's Shop." He looked at a piece of paper. *"I'm going to kill you for this. You're a dead man."*

He glanced up, waiting for my response.

"He slashed my tire then cancelled my credit card and emptied my bank account. I was angry."

"Angry enough to kill?"

We were talking in circles. I'd already been asked this, just in a different way.

"Can I get a cup of water?"

A knock came on the door, and a gorgeous brunette breezed in the room. "Selena Jennings." She nodded to the two sheriffs when they stood. "I represent Rebecca Nichols."

My mouth dropped open. Could this day get any stranger? "You do?"

I'd never seen her before in my life. I didn't even have the cash to call my divorce lawyer for help.

"I'm a friend of Clint's," she said. Stupidly, I experienced a moment of blind jealousy, despite the fact that she was here to help me. She was just so over-the-top beautiful. Why did all his female friends have to be so stunning?

But if she was here, that must mean Clint... what? Cared? That he was here for me even though I was being accused of murder, had no job, no money and there was a dead body in my house? Fresh tears, this time of relief, filled my eyes. If this woman had been sent by Clint, I could let go of some of the panic in my brain. I wasn't alone.

"Clint Tucker, the man you say you were with for the past two nights?" the Meade sheriff asked.

This, too, I'd gone over. The local sheriff had seen us together, even knew Clint personally.

"My client is pregnant," the lawyer said. Every pair of eyes swiveled my way. My scrubs were loose enough to hide my condition, and I was hugging a trash can. "The death of her estranged husband has come as a terrible shock, especially considering he was found in her house, which he should not have had access to. I will make sure she doesn't leave town, but at this point, you've been questioning her for hours. She has an alibi with numerous witnesses from the time Sheriff Duncan saw her until you collected her earlier from her place of employment. Can we wrap it up here?"

Selena conveyed that kind of sexy female authority that made men eager to fall over themselves to please her, and there were enough of them in the room to do just that.

I was just a nauseated woman in lavender scrubs hugging a trash can. The comparison couldn't have been any greater.

Unfortunately, it was still another forty-five minutes before they finished questioning and released me. By that time, I was light-headed from low blood sugar and exhausted. But the moment I stepped out into the lobby, Clint unfolded his long limbs from a chair and came striding forward to meet me. I ran for him and launched myself into his arms.

One hand went to the back of my head, the other cupping my ass as I wrapped my legs around his waist. I didn't care if we were in the lobby, and there were people around. I cried into his neck and practically strangled him, but all he did was hold me and stroke my back.

He was here for me. He'd been waiting.

Finally, after all the tears dried up, I lifted my head.

"Sugar," he said, a smile on his lips.

Only when I nodded did he carry me out of the building and to the parking lot. He and Selena talked as we went.

"I don't give a shit that she has to stay in town. Not happening. I told you where I'm taking her. If they have a problem, deal with it, please."

They spoke more, but I didn't even hear them. I'd lost my ability to focus. I was too exhausted. Too stunned. Too stressed.

I hardly noticed Clint hustling me into his truck. He held up a granola bar, and I nodded. My stomach had settled, and it would stay down. After he opened it for me, I devoured it as we drove toward the canyon. I didn't ask where we were headed. I didn't really care. I just knew Clint would take care of me.

We drove through the Wolf Ranch gates, past the main house and up into the hills. He parked in front of a cabin, similar in look to Audrey and Boyd's, but when he carried me inside and set me on the couch, this time I didn't complain. It wasn't until he carried in a plate of grilled hamburgers that I started to come back to life. I reached for one and shoved it in my mouth like I'd been months without food.

"Oh my God, I was so hungry," I moaned around the bun.

"I know. I'm so sorry, sugar." After I'd eaten about half the burger, I became more aware of my surroundings. The lines of worry in Clint's face. The way he ran his hand over it like he was trying to scrub something away.

"I can't believe he's dead," I said. "I feel bad that I don't really care."

Clint nodded. "Understandable."

I glanced down, picked at my bun. "I thought... I didn't think you'd want to be with me anymore."

His eyes widened then narrowed. "Nothing will keep me away from you, sugar. *Nothing.* You're mine.

Start getting used to it. I'm not giving you or the baby up."

"Clint, I don't want you to feel obligated."

His eyes changed color. I was sure they did, but I didn't have long to notice because he grabbed my plate, set it on the coffee table and yanked me into his arms. His mouth was on mine before I could even gasp.

He settled me, so I was straddling him, his hand on my ass pressing me firmly into him. Into the blatant hard on beneath his jeans. "You think this is an obligation? What I feel for you? How my body craves yours?"

He was breathing hard, his voice ragged. I'd never seen him so out of control, even when Todd was under my window. And yet, his touch was firm but gentle. I felt bound to him in so many ways.

"Clint." I licked my lips.

He growled.

"Fine, not obligation. I want… love. I need it in a relationship. I won't have a life like my parents' lives. The child is the one who suffers. I don't want to be with someone again without it. I know what it's like to be stuck. Trapped."

His hands cupped my face, and I had no choice but to look at him. Only him.

"What the fuck do you think I feel for you?"

"I… I don't know. You've never said," I whispered, my heart beating so loudly in my ears.

"Sugar. I love you. You. Yes, it's crazy. Insane. I know without a doubt you're mine, and I want you forever."

"Clint." This time when I said his name, it was with tears in my eyes. With reverence. "This is insane, but… I tried to push it away. To push you away because it's so intense. So fast."

"Say it," he growled.

"I-I love you."

He stood suddenly and carried me down the hall to the bedroom.

"Clint! What are you doing?"

"The other night, I claimed you." He set me on the bed, crawled over me and tugged at the drawstring of my scrub pants. "You just didn't know it. I'm going to fuck you, so you forget your own name, so you scream mine and know just who you belong to. I'll do it every day of our lives if you need reminding."

18

Clint

"Wait, wait, wait," Becky said, and my wolf nearly howled in disappointment.

The need to satisfy her—to make her feel good after everything that went down today, everything that was *my fucking fault*—was crippling.

"I need a shower first, cowboy. I have to wash this day off me."

Relief filled me, and I smiled. My dick... and my wolf were happy, too.

"I'll help," I offered, picking her up from the bed and carrying her, this time to the bathroom. The cabin had been my grandparents, and they'd given it to me. Rand had inherited a place of his own from our other set of grandparents. We'd said we'd move in when we found our mates. I came to mine on occasion when I wanted to be alone. Living in the bunkhouse was fine most days, but a guy needed room to roam alone sometimes. That was why the place had fresh sheets and had been cleaned recently. I was a bachelor but a tidy one.

The bathroom was small though. It was the first time I'd ever brought a female before, and I looked at the space differently now. Becky would live here, too, and she'd want to make changes. Rustic was fine and all, but not for every day.

"You won't still be carrying me around when I'm nine months pregnant," she said ruefully.

"Wanna bet?" I countered. "I'll be even more inclined to carry you then. Knowing you're pregnant inspires my most primitive instincts. I don't want your feet to ever touch the damn floor again."

She smiled up at me, the weariness on her face starting to lift. Her fingers slid into my hair, and I nearly came from the simple gesture. From receiving affection from my mate. Proof that she was still mine, despite my colossal fuckup.

She loved me despite the truth I was still keeping from her. The secrets.

"I'll be too heavy then."

I shook my head. "Never, sugar. I'm stronger than I look." I winked.

She giggled. "Well, you look pretty strong, so that's saying something."

She didn't know half of it.

I set her on the bathroom counter and turned on the water then returned to undress my mate. She watched me with a soft gaze, letting me strip off her scrub top, lifting her arms over her head to do so. Her bra came off next.

"There they are," I murmured appreciatively when her breasts spilled out.

"I need a bigger bra." She cupped and squeezed them.

I groaned at the sight of her cupping them like an offering. Lush and full, swollen in preparation to feed our pup.

If there was a choice between me being a tits or ass man, I was tits all the way. Although Becky's ass was damned fine, too.

I knocked her hands away.

"Mine," I growled. "My job." I took over, gently massaging them as I lowered my head to flick my tongue over one nipple. It furled against my tongue.

She laughed at my possessiveness, which quickly

turned into a moan. Squirming on the counter, sliding her ass closer to the edge, it was as if she needed to feel me between her legs. So fucking responsive. The room grew steamy and warm as I rubbed the pad of my thumb between her legs, making a wet spot soak through her panties and scrubs. I moved my tongue to the other nipple.

"Clint," she murmured, her pupils dilated, her lower lip trapped between her teeth.

"You're so fucking gorgeous," I murmured, my breath fanning her skin. She smelled so good. Like her own sweet scent, plus her heady arousal and then my scent on her. My dick punched against my jeans, remembering she was mine forever. "This body was made to be worshipped by me."

"I don't want to be worshipped. I want to be fucked." She pulled the snaps open on my shirt and yanked it down my arms. She took a moment, stared at my body. Yeah, the silver wound had finally healed, and she barely gave my side a glance.

I fucking loved the aggression in her. When she shoved her hand into my waistband and used it to yank my hips up into the cradle of her legs, I barely stifled the animal-like growl that came from my throat.

I stamped my mouth down on hers, sucking and

licking my way to heaven. She unbuckled my belt then the button on my jeans.

"Ever been fucked in a shower before?" I broke our frenzied kiss to ask because we weren't going to get much farther than that before I had to get in her.

"No," she admitted. "But if it's as good as against the wall of Cody's storeroom, I'm down."

"Well, that is how we conceived our sweet girl." I picked her ass off the counter and put her down only long enough for us both to shuck the rest of our clothing then I gripped her waist and lifted her hips up to mine. She straddled me, wrapping her legs around my back. In the mirror, I saw her cute feet crossed. "Just think how easily we'll conceive next time if we're horizontal."

She bit my shoulder. Her teeth were blunt and dull compared to a wolf's, but I fucking loved her instinct. I loved that she wanted to bite me back. To mark me like I marked her.

I licked the place my tooth had sunk into her flesh. The spot had a small scab and was slowly healing. "Getting me back?" I teased.

"Uh huh." She glanced up at me through her lashes. "I figure I have lifetime rights. I still don't know how you managed to break skin."

"Weird fluke," I offered, my voice going rusty.

Christ. I *hated* lying to her. Hated holding shit back, especially now when there was literally nothing between us. Especially when she used the word *lifetime* when referring to our relationship.

How much shock could she take in one day? Her ex had been murdered in her house. Finding out her new boyfriend was a wolf might push her over the edge.

Then there was the issue of permanently claiming her without consent. Although after her confession of love tonight, I felt slightly better about springing that on her. Still, now wasn't the time. My dick and wolf both agreed. Fuck now, fuck everything up later.

I set her on her feet in the shower and unwrapped a fresh bar of soap, watching hungrily as she turned in the spray of water and tipped her chin up to wet her hair.

Mine. This female with lush curves and the small swell of our child in her belly. Mine!

I had to continue to reassure myself it was true, despite the fact that I'd marked her. It had happened so quickly, changing my entire life with a chance meeting in the grocery store.

I rolled the bar of soap in my hands to lather it up then stroked my sudsy palm down the side of her neck and over her shoulder, careful to avoid the healing puncture wound. She watched me with water droplets on her lashes as I spread the suds across her sternum, between her breasts then up and around the twin beauties, thumbing her nipples as I worked.

She shuffled her feet on the tub floor like she was trying to rub those sweet inner thighs together. I could scent that she was wet, and from more than just water. I molded my palm to her side and slid it down her waist to her hip then around to knead the soft pillow of her ass.

"I get to play, too." Her voice was husky. She took the soap from my hand and gathered suds to spread across my chest. Her gaze followed her action, and I realized she hadn't had any opportunity to study me before. We were so different. Her soft to my hard. Her gentle roundness to my sharp edges. Her silky skin to my hair covered physique.

Everywhere she touched my skin ignited sparks of pleasure. Of desire. It humbled me. My dick was so hard it throbbed. But it could wait. It always would as Becky always came first. I dropped to my knees and stroked both hands around the globes of her ass then slid one between her knees, working all the way up to her inner thigh without actually touching her sex.

"Clint," she moaned hoarsely, burrowing her fingers in my wet hair and pulling.

Carefully, I turned her so her back was against the tile, extra support so she wouldn't slip. I had her securely, but I would always be protective.

"You need my tongue here?" I asked, lifting the leg I'd been cleaning and putting it over my shoulder. Her heel dug into my back.

"Y-yes. Yes, please."

"Mmm, so polite." I loved that she knew what she wanted and wasn't afraid to tell me. I'd fulfill every one of her fantasies. First, eating pussy. I licked a long line from her anus to her clit. "So fucking sweet." I brought my thumb to her back pucker and massaged a slow circle over the tight ring of muscles as I flicked my tongue repeatedly over her clit.

"Oh," she cried in wanton surprise.

"I think you deserve a reward after what you've been through today."

She massaged my scalp with the fingers of both hands. "I thought there was going to be punishment," she murmured, eyes half closed and hazy.

I grinned up at her. "There can be both, sugar. Punishment and reward."

Excitement blazed in her eyes, and I grinned wickedly as an idea formed. I wasn't about to tell her what it was though.

I returned my attention to her little nubbin, lightly grazing it with my teeth, flicking it. Rubbing my tongue over it in a side-to-side motion. I shifted to my middle finger on her back hole and sank my thumb into her welcoming pussy.

She let out a cry of pleasure, and I pushed her hips back against the shower wall and pinned them there.

The spray shifted away from my face when she moved the showerhead to the side then returned to urging my face against her juicy folds. If she was worried about me getting a little water in my eyes, I wasn't doing my job well enough. I'd fix that.

"You like getting finger fucked in the shower, sugar?" I asked between flicks of my tongue. "Hmm?"

She gripped my ears and tugged. "H-hard to get clean when you're so busy getting dirty," she admonished, and I laughed.

"You haven't seen anything, yet, sweet thing." I pumped my thumb inside her several times then applied pressure with my middle finger and breached her back hole.

"Oh my God!" she cried, half in alarm, half in ecstasy.

She clenched down on both digits then relaxed. Then, I slipped my finger in a little farther then back. A gentle finger fuck of her ass.

"Uh huh. Take your punishment, sugar. When you're naughty, you're going to take it in the ass."

Her pussy contracted again around my thumb, telling me she loved every moment of it, so I kept it up, sucking on her clit, and working my fingers in both holes. I alternated, pushing my thumb in then my middle finger, then I fucked her with both at the same time. I knew it wasn't going to be much of a punishment.

"Oh my God, oh my God, oh my—"

I pulled both fingers out of her and sat back on my heels.

"What?" She blinked down at me. "Oh Clint, I was so close."

I stood up and washed my hands under the water. "I know." I reached down and rubbed her clit ever so lightly. "But this is punishment, remember? Clearly, you like having something in your ass, so that can't be your punishment. Instead, you don't get to come until I decide."

"What?" Some of the glassiness left her eyes as

her already flushed cheeks turned a deeper pink. "No, that's not fair."

I stroked along her dewy slit again, slowly this time, bringing my lips to hers. "Oh, you'll think it's more than fair when I finally let you. I promise, sugar. But until then, you're mine to torture."

She shook her head. "No, no, no, no, no," she moaned, bringing her own fingers to her sex. "I have to come. I'm telling you—"

I captured her wrist and turned her around, gently bending her arm behind her back. It had the effect of pushing her over-sized breasts out and up and made my throbbing dick even harder than it already was. Especially since looking over her shoulder, I got to watch rivulets of water drip off the pert tips. I grabbed a handful of her ass and squeezed. "Don't make me spank you, too. That might hurt me more than you with that precious cargo you're carrying."

Her lust-addled mind must have cleared because her gaze on my face shone with trust and excitement again. "You know that wouldn't hurt anything. The doctor said—"

I dragged my mouth across her nape. "That you could be spanked?" Had she actually asked that exact question?

"Well, not that but any kind of sex was fine."

"Are you saying you want to be spanked?" My dick was pressed between my belly and her lower back, spurting her with pre-cum, although she wouldn't know it.

She wiggled her ass, rubbing it against my eager cock. "Maybe just a little."

I laughed and gave her a swat, keeping it light.

"Harder," she sang.

I smacked the other side, making the flat of my hand more firm, and she gasped then circled her hips with a "Mmmm."

"You like that?" I tried another one then another. When I tested between her legs, she practically gushed with her natural lubricant.

Fates, not getting us both off immediately was going to be a holy torture for me as well.

But worth it. So worth it.

I circled her luscious ass with my hand. "Let's get you out of here." I turned off the water and untwisted her arm, turning her to face me. Then I scooped her up into my arms.

"You're not going to let me walk much, are you?" she asked, but she wasn't put out. She had a smile on her face… and the head of my dick nudging her hip.

"Nope." Yeah, I might have been showing off a

little. It wasn't fair, since she didn't know what I was, yet, but my wolf preened under the sunshine of her appreciation, her admiration.

On my way out of the bathroom, I grabbed a couple towels and draped one over the top of her. "Don't want you getting cold," I said.

"Oh, I don't think there's any chance of that." Her voice was soft with admiration.

I carried her to the wrought iron bed and spread the other towel out before I laid her down. I looked my fill as I slowly slid my fingers over her juicy sex.

19

Becky

CLINT STARED down at me with glittering eyes. They looked silver again, even though the room was well-lit. "You're so beautiful," he said as he looked over every inch of me.

I felt it. He made me feel it. Like most women, I went in and out of feeling confident about my looks. I knew I was pretty cute, but I also knew I was aging out of the cute stage. I was also pregnant and at the weird phase where it wasn't obvious. I looked like I put on weight.

Beautiful wasn't a word I'd been called before.

And I'd certainly never felt like it fit before now. Sure, I shouldn't give a shit. I was making a human… but still. Having Clint look at me with such heat and need… took away all my insecurities.

Lying under Clint's searing gaze with my body curvier with pregnancy, I felt gorgeous.

Desirable. Seeing how hard he was made me feel powerful, too. I did that to him, and it pleased me.

I reached down to touch myself because he stroked me too lazily, but he caught my hand and brought it to his mouth to kiss. "Uh uh, beautiful. You know the rules. I'm in charge of your orgasm tonight."

I had no idea why his bossiness was so hot, but I loved it. My ass still tingled from the spanking. I'd never had anyone do it before. Todd had never been adventurous in bed. Far from it. Thanks to Clint, I was discovering what made me hot. Hell, I'd never had a quickie before him, and I'd gone really wild. It turned out, I liked kinky stuff.

I shook my head but smiled.

"What?" he asked.

"I just figured out I'm a dirty girl."

His eyes widened, and he grinned. "That night at Cody's? You were a hot little thing. Wild."

"For you," I clarified.

"That's right. You're a dirty girl for me. Only me. You want to get your butt spanked? I'll get it nice and pink. As for your ass, don't worry, we'll get my dick in you there."

I gasped, and he dragged the head of his cock through my juices. "Yeah, that idea got you wet."

It had. I was always wet for him.

I sent up a silent thank God.

"This wet pussy's mine. When do you get to come, sugar?"

Oh God, please. I wiggled my hips, trying to get that flared head to sink into me. I rocked my hips down, encouraging him to push in. When he didn't give me what I wanted, I stilled. "When you decide," I answered obediently.

He rewarded me by pushing in making me cry out. "That's right. And whose name are you going to scream when you finally do come?" He arced slowly in and out of me, driving me insane with the tease.

"You," I panted, letting my eyes fall closed. He was so big. So hard. I had no idea how I made it since last night without it inside me. "I mean yours. I'll scream your name."

He sank into the hilt, grinding his flesh over my clit. I squirmed to get more friction, take him deeper.

"Yes," I encouraged, reaching back and gripping his ass, feeling the play of taut muscles as he moved.

He withdrew then punched in again, with a snap, smacking my flesh with his, making a light spanking sound.

"Yes!" I cried out. It was so good. It had never been like this before. Not until Clint. It was as if my body knew it belonged to him. That he was the only one who could make me feel like this.

He grabbed my knees and bent them up, gripping the fronts of my thighs to hold me in place as he fucked with short, quick strokes.

"Okay?" he asked.

I blinked, and he loosened his hold. Through my foggy brain, I realized he was checking on me, making sure he wasn't being too rough.

"More," I moaned as my reply.

He grinned ruthlessly and did some magical hip shift which made my eyes roll back in my head.

So. Good.

Unbelievably good.

If this was what pregnancy sex was like, I was going to stay pregnant for the rest of my life.

Except I already knew. It wasn't the pregnancy. It was the partner. Clint was a *god* when it came to sex.

The very best.

He jackhammered into me with the short, quick thrusts, and I moaned with pleasure.

And then he pulled out.

"Clint!" I pushed up on my elbows, tears of sexual frustration stabbing my eyes. "You're killing me. Literally killing me."

"Is that a fact?" he drawled although it couldn't be that comfortable for him, either. His erection jutted out, hard as a flag pole and glistening with my arousal. He rolled my knees all the way back to my shoulders, spreading me wide and presenting my sex. He entered me from this position, which was intense right from the beginning.

"Oh," I gasped. "Oh, oh, oh."

I was so close. All it would take would be one swipe of my clit, and I'd go off. But now I found myself wanting to play Clint's game. Not coming until he gave me permission. What did he have planned?

I didn't even know where he learned to play such a game, and I certainly wanted to stab the eyes out of the woman he'd practiced it with before, but damn. It certainly was fun.

He pulled out again, as I'd suspected he would. Gah! My whole body was aflame now, nipples hardened to diamond points, clit hard and throbbing, pussy pulsing.

Clint rolled me to my belly and pushed my thighs open.

"Is this comfortable for you?"

Damn him for being considerate. "Just fuck me already. I promise I'll let you know if something's not working for me."

"All right, sugar."

He gave me a light swat on the ass then he parted my buttcheeks. I clenched my anus with a shiver.

His tongue found my back hole, swirling around it. I gasped.

It was so dirty. The feeling was so intense but felt so good. I had no idea.

At least I was clean from the shower. That was all I could think before thought dissolved into total pleasure. Total surrender.

"Clint," I moaned, agitation building and building in my core.

He lifted his head and slapped my right cheek once more.

"Ohh," I warbled.

He brought his thumb to my anus and massaged until I loosened the ring of muscles and let him in.

Again—so dirty. So taboo. And yet the pleasure was over-the-top. More intense than vaginal. Definitely weird. But so good.

When he scooped an arm under my waist and lifted me to my knees, it got even hotter. He entered me from behind, his thumb still buried in my ass.

I rolled my face in the bedcovers, moaning, eyelids fluttering, jaw slack. The wash of sensation was almost too much.

I held still, biting the bedspread as he pumped in and out of me, working his thumb at the same time. My panting increased, a feverish heat spread through my entire body. "Clint!" I screamed.

"That's right, sugar. You come now. And keep screaming my name." He plowed into me four more times and then sank deep with a shout.

I started coming the moment he gave me permission, and he was right. The orgasm that ripped through my body was like no other I'd ever experienced. My muscles squeezed and clenched around his shaft, my anus contracted around his thumb, and I reached beneath me to rub my own clit. It was possible I lost my mind for a minute. Maybe five. Maybe thirty.

It was a long time before my brain cleared enough for me to remember where I was. Who I was. All I knew was how good I felt. My entire body buzzed and hummed with my release, pleasure coursing through my veins.

Clint eased out of both my holes and left to wash his hands. He returned with a warm washcloth and cleaned me up. I hadn't moved from the prostrate position. I was still on my knees with my chest pressed against the mattress. Clint eased me to my side and wrapped his longer body around mine from behind. He moved my damp hair and kissed my nape.

"Becky?"

I made a funny grunting sound in reply.

"Sugar, I need to tell you something." His arm draped over my waist and pulled me close.

It was hard to tug myself out of my euphoria, but I managed a "hmm?" That was a little more coherent.

I heard him swallow behind me and a sliver of unease crept in. "The guys on the ranch—Boyd and Colton and Rob. Me and my family... we're, ah, different."

I laced my fingers over his and pulled them against my chest. "Different how?"

He was quiet for a moment and a niggling of fear crept in. What was he trying to say?

I turned to face him, to look into his eyes when

he spoke about something that was obviously really important.

That was when the front door was kicked in.

20

Clint

My wolf instincts had me grabbing Becky and rolling us to the far side of the bed, away from the bedroom doorway. We dropped to the floor, and I tucked, so I hit the hard wood, and she was protected from the fall with my body. Only then did I flip us and, as much as I could, set her as far beneath the bed as possible. I heard the frantic beating of her heart and felt the goosebumps rise on her skin. Her fingers clutched at me like talons, yet I had to set her from me. Only when she was hidden and as safe as possible, did I jump up and leap across the bed.

I heard the heavy footsteps of the intruder, the ragged breathing. Taking a deep breath of my own, I couldn't miss the tang of sweat beneath the obvious scent of shifter. The cold, outside air pushed it toward me. Only an enemy would enter unannounced. Any shifter within a hundred feet of the cabin would have heard us fucking, known I would be vulnerable.

My adrenaline pumped, my wolf at the ready. Shifters in wolf form didn't come through the front door. I would fight like for like except I was naked. I had no weapons. I had my gun in the truck, but that would do me no good now. The only way to fight would be in wolf form, but then I wouldn't be able to protect Becky.

Fuck! I'd known Donald would come. That was why we hadn't stayed at the house in town. Here, we had protection. Rob and I had put a plan together, but that had been before Becky's ex's murder. We'd changed plans, so we'd stay here under watch, under pack guard. In town, this couldn't be done.

I'd been fucking stupid. Donald's need for revenge had escalated. He'd killed a human, just like his cousin, without care that the human police would investigate. It had been a sign to tell me he could get close to my mate, but he'd broken pack law. The same as Jarod.

"Enforcer!" The voice carried into the room a second before a man stood in the doorway. It was dark, but I saw him as clear as day. He wore no coat, only a dirty thermal shirt and jeans. Heavy boots on his feet. His long brown hair shot out wild about him. As wild as his deep yellow gaze. His wolf was showing.

So was the gun in his hand.

Rob was watching the road by the ranch—the only entrance to this mountain. But Donald must've slipped past him.

"Donald." I kept my voice low. Even. I'd never met the fucker before, but there was no one else who he could be.

"You killed my cousin. Put a bullet in his head."

"He broke pack law. Robbed convenience stores and murdered innocent humans."

"We take care of our own," he countered. He tipped his chin down to stare even more intently.

I had to stall him, keep his attention on me, off Becky. He'd know she was here. The scent of her, my cum and her arousal was heavy in the air. With the front door open, the room was getting colder by the minute. I could barely feel it, but I knew Becky would begin to chill.

"I don't make the decisions. I just follow orders. The council's judgement was delivered and completed."

"You killed him," he seethed. Spittle fell from his lips, and he used his empty hand to wipe it away.

"I did." I heard Becky's slight intake of breath, and I kept talking to cover it, but Donald's gaze flicked to the unmade bed. "Shifter justice is my job."

"You didn't even fight him like a wolf. You ended him in human form. You put a bullet in Jarod's head. Your mate will get the same fate. Then you'll know how it feels to have someone you love taken from you. To live yet be dead inside."

Oh Fates. He wasn't here for me. *He was here for Becky.*

"You went to her house to kill her," I realized out loud.

Todd wasn't the intended target.

"She wasn't there, but the male human was, taking her TV. He saw me break in, knew my face. He had to die."

Todd's asshole ways had gotten him killed. If he'd just left Becky alone, he'd be living his miserable life in Meade. But he'd had to keep fucking with her, and he'd had his throat ripped out.

If I hadn't kept her with me, she'd have been at home. He'd have broken in, and she'd have been defenseless against Donald. In human form and especially as a wolf.

A growl rumbled deep in my chest at the thought of her dying at this asshole's sick idea of vengeance.

"You're just like your cousin." I tried to keep his focus on me. If he shot me, I'd survive. Not if he shot me in the head, but he had lots of other places to aim for. "You both went rogue. You bring danger to our kind. You'll be put down like him."

His body tensed. Every muscle practically quivered. "Enough! She dies."

He stepped toward the bed, arm extended with his weapon pointed in front of him. Before I even knew what I was doing, I leapt over the corner of the bed and picked him up with shifter strength. No, more than shifter strength. It was shifter with an endangered mate strength. The power coursing through my limbs went beyond what I knew I was capable of. When I threw him, he flew across the room and crashed through the bedroom window.

Glass shattered as he fell through and onto the snow-covered ground outside.

"Stay inside, Becky. Don't come out," I warned and dived out the window after him. He would be on his feet quickly. I needed Becky inside with Donald out. Bullets wouldn't go through the log walls.

I tucked and rolled, bumping and scraping over rocks and fallen branches, coming back to my feet. Glass probably cut me, but I couldn't feel it. I was solely focused on Donald.

The wind whipped around us, my feet sunk deep in snow up to my ankles. Headlights cut across the trees as several vehicles sped in and skidded to stop at the cabin. My pack had my back.

Thank fuck. I didn't know how they knew to come, but thank fuck. One of them would protect Becky while I finished this shit.

A shot rang out. It went wide, but chips of wood flew from the bullet hitting a tree to my right, nicking my skin.

"Can't even shoot a gun," I taunted. "Can you even shift?"

I wanted him in wolf form. I wasn't an alpha, but I'd been made an enforcer for a reason. Threats like him had to be ended. The battle was to the death. I was prepared for it every time I'd gone out and hunted a rogue shifter. This time, it was different.

This time, I was protecting my mate. My unborn child.

I couldn't save them in human form. I had to get him to shift.

He did. Angry as he was, his wolf had pushed forward, taken over. He probably couldn't even resist the pull. He crouched and the sounds of shifting, of bone and muscle rearranging, then the renting of fabric filled the air. The gun fell uselessly into the snow.

His wolf was tan. While big, he wasn't as large an animal as I was.

I stalked toward him, shifting at the same time. By the time I was on four paws, he was turning tail and running away. Going after him, I herded him to the far side of the cabin to the open clearing. I wanted room to fight, room for others to arrive, to witness the elimination of the threat to my mate.

I had no idea if the council had passed judgement on Donald or only sent an enforcer to keep an eye on him. It didn't matter now. He'd admitted to killing Todd. That was enough to have him finished.

I wasn't an enforcer here and now. I was a male whose mate had been threatened. We protected what was ours fiercely, and I was within my rights as mate alone to end Donald's life.

Any male shifter would do the same.

I leaped on him, rolling us several times until he was beneath me. I bit his flank, and his wolf pushed me off. We circled, snarled. I tasted his blood on my tongue. It dripped from my teeth.

As we moved, I saw Rob walk out of the darkness to stand in the periphery. Rand did as well. Then Colton and a male I'd never seen before. I assumed he was the enforcer. They stood sentinel, arms crossed, legs spread. Doing nothing but watching. No one would take this from me.

This was my fight. My battle.

Out of the corner of my eye, I caught a glimpse of Becky. Shit! I didn't want her out here, seeing this. She stood with Boyd—his arm around her shoulders—in the cabin's doorway. She was wrapped in the blanket from the bed and had her boots on her feet.

Donald launched at me, his fangs sinking into my leg. The pain of his sharp bite shot through me, but I rolled, got free. Put my body between my mate and the vengeful wolf.

"Clint." Her wobbling voice cut through the darkness, straight into my chest.

Goddammit. I didn't want Becky watching. Didn't want her to find out about us this way. To see what I was about to do.

Fuck—why did Boyd let her witness this? She was safe with him, with the others in a large circle around us. But Becky wouldn't understand.

I was not human.

I was a shifter. A black wolf. I was a killer in both forms. Now she knew it all from the words Donald and I had shared and again in action. And I had to kill again. In front of her.

I had to see it done. She and the baby would be safe. Even if she never forgave me for what I am and what I've done.

It was over for Donald. He just didn't know it yet.

As for me, it was over, too. I knew it all too well.

21

Becky

WHAT THE FUCK? *What. The fuck?*

I couldn't process what was happening. One minute, we were in bed, the soft hazy afterglow of wild sex surrounding us. The next, I was rolled onto the floor and practically shoved beneath the bed because someone had kicked in the front door.

Clint had acted so quickly. His instincts to protect me were strong. As I'd laid there... *naked*, I had to wonder if he'd acted so fast because he'd been expecting it.

Who was anticipating someone kicking their way into your house?

This wasn't a big city. We weren't even in Cooper Valley. We were above Wolf Ranch in the flipping mountains. There were no houses, no people around for miles. In fact, the nearest place was probably Audrey and Boyd's or the main house. If any of them came to visit, they'd knock.

I'd gone from stunned and confused to stunned and scared. The guy... Donald... had accused Clint of some really bad things. Shooting his cousin in the head? I'd expected Clint to deny it, to say there was a mistake. He hadn't.

He'd admitted it.

Clint was a murderer. The crazed guy, the one who I hadn't even seen since I was shoved under the bed, had every reason for revenge. As I'd laid there, I hadn't been able to reconcile the Clint I knew from the Clint this guy described. The way only minutes before he'd been inside me, coaxing an orgasm from my body.

Way back at the bachelorette party, he'd hoisted that handsy guy up by the throat but hadn't done more. He hadn't even defended himself or fought back when he'd gotten his nose broken. With Todd the other night at my house, he'd done the same lift-by-the-throat move but hadn't hurt him. With me, Clint had always been gentle... except when I hadn't wanted him to be. But even then, he'd checked in with me.

But murder?

Things went from bad to worse when Donald stated he planned to kill me. A death for a death. Was this what Clint had been expecting? Was this why he'd shoved me behind the bed to be protected?

That had all been crazy, but it had gone from that to insane.

They'd fought and gone out the window like in a movie. When I realized they weren't coming back, I tugged the sheet from the bed and wrapped it around myself and ran into the front room to watch from the other window. It was then I saw Donald's dark form change to a wolf.

It was night. It was dark. There were no streetlights. But the moon was out, and the snow made it bright. I couldn't miss the outline of the men against the stark white ground. He'd changed from human to wolf.

Yes, a *fucking wolf*. Then Clint had done the same thing. I blinked. Then again.

I stared, trying to process what I knew I'd seen when they loped off out of view.

I ran to the front door and stifled a scream when I bumped into someone. Big hands gripped my upper arms, and I began to fight. "It's Boyd, darlin'. Shh, it's okay."

I stilled. "He's a wolf," I muttered, holding the blanket snug around me.

"Yeah, darlin', he is," Boyd replied. "You're safe now. You're not hurt, are you? The baby okay?"

I heard snarls and movement outside, but Boyd blocked my view.

"I'm... I'm fine. Why aren't you helping? Stop them. Something."

"Nah, Clint's got it under control."

Under control? "I... I don't know what that even means."

"That guy, Donald, is a danger." Snarls filled the air, and I shivered.

"He said he killed Todd, that he wanted to kill me," I said, staring at the front of his coat. "For revenge."

A growl rumbled from Boyd's chest. "Like I said, Clint will take care of him."

My stomach roiled. "I need to see."

He sighed, not letting go of me. "That's not a good idea. It's gonna get—"

"Clint's going to kill him, isn't he?"

"Donald threatened his mate. His unborn child."

Mate. Boyd must mean me.

"He said... he said Clint was an enforcer."

Boyd stilled, and his fingers tightened on my arms. "Holy shit. That fucking makes sense."

I blinked. "I don't understand. What's an enforcer? Why are they *wolves?*"

Boyd bent down, so we were eye to eye. "Darlin', we all are. And that baby of yours? Probably will be, too."

I tried to step out of his hold. Boyd, a wolf?

"Now, don't be scared," he said, his voice soft as if placating a child. "You know we'd never hurt you. We're here to keep you safe. That's what Clint's doin' out there right now."

"No." I shook my head and tried to pull away again. "This is nuts. I—" I wrenched away from him. "Let me see," I said with fierce determination.

"Clint won't want you to watch this."

"*Clint* doesn't have any say," I snapped.

"Fuck," he whispered then studied me. "You sure? It's gonna be pretty gruesome. I think it's best if you—"

"I *have* to see. I have to know what Clint is." Everyone knew. Everyone knew Clint was a wolf but me. I'd been in the dark this whole time. The father of my child wasn't even *human.* So no, I wasn't letting Boyd control what I learned about Clint.

"Audrey's gonna kill me. But all right. Got some boots? Yeah, there they are." He brought them over to me, dropped them on the floor and took my hand to balance. "Tuck your feet in them, all right. Come on."

I pushed past him and ran outside, past the front door hanging off its hinges. Boyd caught up and kept his arm around me as we watched. Two wolves circling, fighting. Snarling. Biting. Clint was the black one—massive and terrifying. They weren't like any wolves I'd seen before. They were both oversized. Ferocious.

Clint lunged and pinned the brown wolf. He went for his throat. A high-pitched yelp pierced the air. Blood splattered the snow and the animal lay still. Clint had won. He killed the other wolf.

I turned and threw up off the side of the porch.

And then I ran. I ran back inside and threw on my clothes. My hands shook so badly I could barely make my fingers work.

Boyd followed me at first, I thought, but of

course, when I dropped the sheet and started dressing, he shut the bedroom door and waited on the other side. I hardly noticed the tears coursing down my cheeks.

I just wanted to leave. Get the hell away from this crazy scene. This unbelievable unfolding. Clint was a wolf. Boyd was a wolf. I'd seen Rob, Colton and Rand standing around watching as we had. I had to assume they became wolves, too. What about Audrey and the other ladies? God, I'd been so dumb. So blind.

Jesus. I'd thought Todd was bad? At least he was human. And least he didn't tear out throats with his teeth while his friends stood around watching.

These people had lied to me—all of them.

I threw open the bedroom door, smacking Boyd with it. "Is Audrey..."

"No," Boyd said quickly, putting an arm around my shoulders again. I shrugged him off. "No, she's human like you. Marina, too. You look like you're bolting, and that's not a good idea right now. Let me take you to Audrey. She can help talk you through some of this."

I swiped at my nose. My mouth tasted like bile. "Yeah. Fine."

Anything to get away from there.

To not have to speak to Clint. Or acknowledge what he was. To not see the life he'd just taken.

It was too much.

It was all too much.

Boyd led me outside, and I avoided looking anywhere but right in front of my feet. I threw up again behind Boyd's truck.

As I sat in the passenger seat, Clint came running up—naked, covered in blood. When he saw my face, he stopped. His eyes were wide and wild, but he looked… savage, and that scared the hell out of me.

He was the man I'd said I loved. He was the man whose child I was carrying.

"Drive away," I snapped at Boyd, my chin quivering.

"I'm sorry," Clint said through the glass. From the expression on his face, I believed him. He looked positively haunted. Of course, that could be the blood that coated his lips and chin. "I wanted to tell you."

I forced myself to look away.

I couldn't. How had I done this to myself again?

The pain in my chest just kept getting sharper with every passing breath.

I needed to get away from him.

To think.

I needed this to be over.

"Go!" I shouted, and Boyd finally put his foot on the gas, and we took off, wheels spinning.

22

CLINT

I DROPPED to my knees in the snow as Boyd's truck departed with my mate and pup.

I would've called out to her, but I had no air left in my lungs. She'd taken it all with her.

The look on her face.

Fuck.

Tipping my chin back, I looked up at the black night and bellowed. I might have ripped the throat out of Donald, but my mate had ripped my heart from my chest.

I would never forget that look as long as I lived.

Pale. Sickened. Unbelievably hurt.

I couldn't have fucked this up worse. I'd just killed a man in front of her. No, I'd killed a wolf. The first time she saw my wolf, and it was in a fight to the death.

I'd always known my job as council executioner would end my life early. I just hadn't known it would be from heartbreak.

Losing a mate I'd never believed I could have.

Before I ever really had her. And a family.

"Come on, buddy, let's get you in the cabin." Two guys hauled me up by my arms—Rob and Rand. Rob spoke with a low, authoritative growl, but I barely heard it. Barely registered.

"Mate," I murmured through numb lips.

"Boyd will take care of your mate," Rand promised. "I still don't understand why that shifter was here. And what did he have to do with Becky?"

I could barely move my legs to get into the cabin. They all but shoved me into the shower, and Rob turned on the spray. It was cold, but I didn't feel it. I went through the quick motions of getting the blood and mud off me then stepped out to dry off. I found clothes on the vanity, and I put them on then went out and dropped on the couch. Rob, Rand, Colton and a shifter I'd never met were waiting. I smelled coffee. Someone must have started a pot.

"You gonna fill us in now?" Rand demanded, tossing a sweatshirt at me. I let it lay where it landed in my lap.

I glanced at Rob, who nodded.

"I'm a council enforcer," I said. "Well, I was."

The room went still. "You knew this?" Colton demanded of Rob then muttered, "Of course, you did."

"Fuck, brother. For how long?" Rand asked. He sat in one of the kitchen chairs.

"Years."

"Do Mom and Pop know?"

I shook my head. "Only Rob, until now."

"Jesus, no wonder you're so fucking... chill when you're home."

"Thanks," I said, not feeling it.

"That guy was someone you'd been tracking?" Rand asked, leaning forward and propping his elbows on his thighs.

I shook my head then dropped it into my hands, elbows propped on my knees.

Rob took over explaining. "Clint carried out a council execution last week—shifter who'd been murdering convenience store workers in Wyoming."

"I heard about that," Colton said.

Rob nodded then leaned against the counter, as if

settling in with his tale. "This was his cousin, Donald, who was after Becky to make Clint suffer, but Donald ran into her ex at her place first and killed him."

"Fuck, I heard about that, too," Colton added, taking off his hat and rubbing his head.

"Then Donald somehow found Clint up here." Rob came over, dropped a hand on my shoulder. "I'm sorry, bro. I don't know how he found you. No vehicles came up the road past the ranch."

"I've been tracking him by scent," the stranger in the room said.

Everyone looked at him. It wasn't like I'd been ignoring the guy, but I knew he was an enforcer, and I wasn't going to out him. I also wasn't going to ask his name. The less I knew, the safer it was for him.

"I'm Ben Davies," he offered. "The council sent me."

"Another enforcer?" Colton asked, dark brow raised.

"That's not for us to know," Rob reminded him.

Colton huffed out a laugh.

Rand stood and went over to shake the guy's hand then dropped back into his chair.

"I got his scent over at your mate's house," Davies said. "He must've been there in wolf form."

"He ripped my mate's ex's throat out."

Davies nodded. "Makes sense then. I followed it to a motel by the highway. Then it cut up into the mountains. I've been trailing it all night. When I realized it led to the cabin where Rob said you'd be, I called him for reinforcements."

I should've said *thank you*. I knew I should've, but I couldn't make my lips work. None of it mattered —*none of it*—with Becky gone.

No, that wasn't true. Donald was dead. I'd protected her from him. She was safe with Boyd. My pup was safe. That was important. But she'd left. She wanted nothing to do with me, and it made me want to howl at the moon again.

"All these years... all those trips. That's where you were going?" Rand asked.

"Yeah." I spoke into my hands. I forced myself to lift my head and look at him. He was my younger brother. The kid who'd looked up to me. Who'd tried to emulate me. And now he was finding out I put down rogue shifters. That I'd lied for years. "Do you hate me, too?"

Rand scoffed. "No, way, Clint. You just moved up four notches in my book. You're the guy who does the dirty work, so the rest of us can stay blissfully ignorant. Like Colton with the Green

Berets." He thumped his chest with his fist. "Respect."

I bowed my head again. I didn't give a shit about respect if Becky had none for me. "My mate's gone." I said it out loud to the whole group of shifters.

Yeah, I was a fucking pansy. But I'd just had my heart ripped out by the female who'd made it beat in the first place.

"This was probably a shock to her," Colton said. "Give her some time and space. She'll come around."

Would she, though?

She'd been clear with me about not wanting anything messy. She'd already had enough drama for a lifetime with Todd. Now I was responsible for Todd's death. I'd kept secrets from her about who I was and worse—what I did for a living. It was my fault she'd been in danger even though I told her she was safe with me. The complete opposite was true.

Todd had been a liar. I was a liar. Todd had been an asshole. I had a darkness in me that wasn't going to go away. A past filled with death. She'd witnessed it firsthand. I might walk away from being an enforcer, but it was a stain that could never fade from my soul. For a shifter like Rand, he could feel proud. For a human like Becky, she was repulsed.

I wasn't sure we'd recover from that.

I wanted to hop in my truck and go to her, but getting pushy now wasn't going to fix things. No, I had no choice but to let her go, even though it made my wolf howl like he'd never stop. I stood, kicked the coffee table, which flipped over, landing on the hardwood. I probably broke my toe, for the pain shot all the way up past my shin.

"Easy," Rob said, his voice low and deep. The alpha in him was trying to calm me, but it wasn't helping.

"I'm not needed here any longer. I assume I can pass on your resignation to the council?" Davies asked, zipping his coat.

I nodded. "I'm done."

"I'll take care of the body." He nodded to Rob then left. Since the front door was still hanging by a hinge, he didn't close it behind him.

"It's going to kill me and my wolf not to be near her, protecting. Providing," I told the guys. Rand was my blood, but Colton and Rob were brothers just the same.

"Time and space," Colton said again. "Human women are stubborn as fuck."

"I'm going to find a nice, mild she-wolf and settle down without all the bullshit you all faced," Rand declared.

"Good luck with that," I countered. Whomever Rand's wolf chose as a mate would take him for one hell of a run.

"I agree with Colton," Rob said. "Boyd won't let anything happen to her. Hell, he's going to be stuck with two pregnant humans carrying shifter babies. I pity him."

I could only imagine him hunting down avocados and whatever weird food Audrey craved.

"Audrey will be your biggest ally, brother," Rand said.

Rob and Colton both nodded. "She'll be able to explain things better than anyone else."

Fuck. I had to rely on a human female to guide my mate in shifter ways.

It should be my job. My right. It killed me knowing I may never get that privilege. To share with her the joy of having a wolf within. Of being with a mate who would do anything for her.

I'd watch over her. I'd protect her. At least not up close. I might be relegated to protecting and providing from afar. Begging for glimpses of her, scraps of time with the pup.

Oh fuck.

How would I ever survive without her?

23

Becky

I DIDN'T WANT to be at Audrey's. I didn't know where I wanted to be. Certainly not my house where Todd had been murdered. God, he'd had his throat ripped out by that wolf I just saw bleed out in the snow. I never wanted to go to my place again.

I felt as if everyone I knew, everyone I thought I cared about, led a secret life. Todd and his underhanded plans for me. Clint, obviously. Even my best friend knew about shifters and hadn't said anything. Hell, just the other night, we'd gabbed around Willow's table about my relationship with

Clint, and *none* of them had said a word. Not Rob when he'd let us in. Not Audrey, Marina or Willow all the time I'd stuffed my face with snacks.

They must have been laughing at me when I left. How did I look Audrey in the eye?

Then there was the whole shifter thing. Holy fuck, I'd never seen that coming. What the hell was that about? Was it just the guys around the ranch... holy shit. *Wolf. Ranch.*

It was right there all along.

I was so confused. My stomach ached from throwing up twice. I felt like my heart was breaking in two, and my brain was frazzled. I didn't know what to even think. I couldn't bear to talk or listen to anyone right now, either.

Boyd pulled up in front of their cute little cabin, extra adorable in the snow, glowing indoor lights making it all quaint and cozy. He hopped out, came around and escorted me inside.

It reminded me of the times Clint carried me about. *Fuck.*

Audrey rushed to my side when she saw my teary face. She wore black leggings, a hoodie sweatshirt and fleece socks. She was about six weeks further along than me, and her pregnancy couldn't be hidden any longer. Her glasses were perched on her nose, and she looked at me with her usual frown when she was concerned.

"Becky?" She set her hand on my shoulder. "What happened? What's going on?"

"Turns out Clint's been a council enforcer," Boyd said. "A wolf showed up for revenge—the one who killed Becky's ex."

Audrey gasped, and her fingers squeezed.

Boyd sighed before he went on. "He showed up at Clint's family cabin. Kicked the door in and, from what I understand, planned to kill Becky as payback."

"Oh my God." Audrey lifted her hand to her mouth as she studied me.

"She saw her mate shift for the first time. Shift and kill."

Audrey blinked. "Wait, hold up. What's a shifter council enforcer?"

She looked to me, as if the *shift and kill* part was totally normal. Her question confirmed Audrey knew about shifters but not everything.

"Why didn't you tell me?" I broke in, my vision swimming. Really. "I considered you my friend. I mean, girls tell each other important shit. I sure would've liked a heads-up that the man who got me pregnant wasn't a man at all. That my life is now out of a weird horror film."

"I'm sorry," Audrey said, regret etching the lines in her face. Tears filled her eyes, and she blinked them away. "I couldn't tell you about shifters in general. It's the rule. Even if I could, I thought it was Clint's job to tell you what he is. You two were so new, he was probably waiting for the right moment." She took my hand and tugged me to an overstuffed armchair. "Here, sit down. I'll answer all the questions I can, and Boyd will, too. Or he can leave if you just want girl talk."

She pulled a blanket from the couch and draped it around me.

I sniffed, looked up at the two of them as they loomed over me. Boyd really did look concerned. Not once since he'd come into Clint's cabin did he have his usual swagger about him.

"He can stay. We still don't know what the whatever-council-enforcer thing is."

Boyd sat on the couch facing me although watching as if I might freak out again. Or throw up.

"Are you feeling okay? The baby? No cramping or anything?" Audrey asked, eyeing me now like a doctor.

I shook my head.

"Do you need a snack?"

"She threw up twice," Boyd told her, and I glared.

"Lemon tea?" she asked.

That did sound kind of good. "Sure."

Audrey stepped into the kitchen, and I heard her fill the electric kettle and flick it on.

She came back and sat down beside Boyd, leaning against him. He settled his arm around her shoulder, so her head was tucked into him.

"The Shifter Council is sort of the regulating organization for shifters. Like the Supreme Court. Issues go before them, and they make rulings which enforcers carry out. Their identities—the enforcers—are kept secret because they're essentially executioners. They put down shifters who've gone rogue. Usually it's over killing a human. Sometimes it's because they've gone feral—like in the case of moon madness. But an enforcer's job would be to track and kill."

Again, I tried to reconcile the notion of Clint as a killer with the man I'd thought I'd known. Fresh tears tracked down my cheeks. "But Clint…" I shook my head. "He doesn't seem like" —I had to swallow hard over the tight band constricting my throat— "a killer."

Boyd scrubbed a hand over his face. "I didn't know either. I swear. Clint's the most level-headed, kindest one of all of us. Which is probably why he was asked to serve. Why he's quiet. He would've served at Rob's behest." Boyd flicked a glance at me. "Rob's our alpha," he said, as if that explained everything. "The one who leads all the wolves in this area. The pack."

I shook my head to ward off all this information. This whole world I hadn't known existed until tonight. I tucked the blanket around me which prompted Audrey to get up and make my tea.

"Clint kills people for a living?" My teeth chattered from the shock. Audrey returned and pressed a mug in my hands.

"I know it sounds terrible," Boyd admitted. "Human laws wouldn't work on shifters. You couldn't keep us in prisons because we'd just break out. We'd have to run, especially with the moon. And once a shifter's had the taste of human blood, he has to be put down. It'll turn him feral, for sure. They lose their human half and become all beast. They're a danger to humans and shifters alike."

I forced myself to sip the tea which was tangy and hot. It slid down nicely and settled, warming me from the inside out. The lemon cut the bad taste in my mouth, and my stomach didn't mind it, especially empty.

"H-he didn't tell me." Except I remembered what he'd said right before the front door had been kicked in.

The guys on the ranch—Boyd and Colton and Rob. Me and my family... we're, ah, different.

He'd been about to tell me they were wolves. Would he have told me he was an enforcer, too?

I swallowed. "So, everyone on the ranch, you're all wolves?"

Boyd nodded then glanced down at Audrey. The look he gave her made my heart hurt. It was so full of love, of something I'd thought I'd had with Clint. "All the males. Audrey and Marina aren't. Willow is."

For some reason, I remembered the pretty juice girl from the grocery store. "And Clint's cousin, Shelby? His whole family. Janet and Tom. God, Rand, too. Even Nash? Everyone was in on it?"

Boyd sighed. "No one's in on anything. Yes, it was kept from you but not because of anything other than you're human. Clint was going to tell you, I'm sure of it."

I pursed my lips then took another sip of tea.

"Tell them the science behind it," Audrey told Boyd.

He smiled at her. "The part you like, Doctor." He turned his attention back to me. "We're a species, so being a shifter's hereditary. Your baby and Audrey's will carry the genes. Whether they'll have enough of them to actually shift or not will be unknown until adolescence."

I placed my hand on my belly. Anger shot through me. Clint had given me a *werewolf* baby?

But no, he hadn't meant to get me pregnant at all. That had been an accident.

The place he'd bitten me suddenly tingled, and I touched it.

Boyd nodded at my movement, like he knew what I was touching. "Clint marked you. Bit you, right?"

I nodded then blushed, remembering when exactly.

"It's what male wolves do when they've found their true mate. We embed our scent into their skin to keep other males away."

"What?" I set the mug of tea on the end table and stood up. "This is… this is just crazy. He had no right to do that."

Boyd shook his head. "He probably couldn't help himself, Becky," he said gently. "It's instinct. When a shifter finds his one true mate, the biology is overwhelming. We can't hold back. With you being pregnant, his need to protect you would be off the charts." He glanced at his own wife—*mate*—with soft eyes, as if he spoke from experience.

"Wolves mate for life, honey," Audrey said, also standing and hovering nearby. "Clint knew the minute he saw you—he belonged to you."

I shook my head. "No, he didn't. We had a quickie at Cody's. We parted ways. For four months."

"Yeah, but you said his nose was broken. When was the next time you met up?"

"The grocery store. I threw up on him."

"What did he do then?" Audrey asked with a smile.

"He got me out of there, took me home."

"He caught your scent then. Been protective ever since? Bossy?"

I nodded.

"They're all that way," Audrey added.

"Hey!" Boyd said, pretending to take offense.

I whirled on her and frowned. "Yeah, I already had a husband who thought that way. It's not a selling point, Audrey," I snapped.

When she blanched, a kick of remorse went through me. But no. She kept this from me, too.

They all did.

"I'm leaving," I said, even though I had nowhere to go. I didn't even have my car here.

Boyd jumped up. "Clint would want you to stay here."

I narrowed my eyes. "*Clint* has no say," I snarled.

He held up his hands then pulled out his keys. "Okay. Where can I take you? I'd rather you stay here just for my own protective streak, but with that guy... dead, you're safe. You want to stay at Audrey's place in town? Until the police have finished with your house?"

The tight knot in my stomach twisted. None of this felt right.

None of it.

"Yes, please," I said tightly. What choice did I have? "I'd appreciate that."

"I'll come, too," Audrey offered, but Boyd and I both waved her away.

"You and the baby need to stay here. Get some rest, darlin'," Boyd said, his expression going soft again, the way it always did when he looked at her. "I'll get her settled."

Settled.

Fuck that.

My ex was dead. I was a fucking widow. I wasn't sure if I had a job after being taken away for questioning by the police from the hospital. I still might be charged in a murder case. I'd almost been murdered myself. I found out the guy I loved was part wolf. And an executioner. Not only with a bullet to the brain but with his teeth. The baby I was carrying was not fully human. My heart had been obliterated for believing in someone. Trusting them.

No, I didn't think I'd ever feel settled again.

24

Clint

Boyd called me last night. Told me Becky was physically fine. She hadn't been hurt when I'd rolled her to the floor. She and the baby were well. He'd told me they'd tried to explain shifter things to Becky, but she'd been more bitter than receptive. He'd driven her into town and settled Becky into Audrey's house in town. I knew where it was. Knew Boyd had secured that fucker up tight. Audrey rarely stayed there now, only when she was on call, and it was too far to get to the hospital quickly from the ranch. Usually, Boyd stayed with her, but on rare occasions, she crashed alone after a late delivery. I'd even helped him install the top-of-the-line security system.

Becky was safe but alone.

My wolf didn't stand for that shit. I didn't either, but I wasn't going to kick her door in either. Once in her lifetime was enough.

I'd texted her last night that I was sorry I'd kept things from her. That I was sorry I put her in danger. I asked if we could talk, and she'd told me not to call. I had to respect that. I remembered what Rob had said about giving her time and space, but it fucking killed me to be estranged from her. Like I literally felt my body withering away like it would die.

So now I sat across the street in my truck. Watched. It had been quiet all night. Clouds had come in and covered the moon. Snow began to fall. Yeah, I spent the night in my truck. No, I didn't give a fuck about the cold.

Dawn came, and I'd seen no movement from the house. Boyd pulled up a little after seven. He got out, and I rolled down my window. Snow quickly settled on the brim of his hat. He tucked up the collar on his coat. "Just dropped Audrey at the hospital. Go home. Get some rest. Hell, go up in the hills and run. I'll watch her."

My wolf was resistant, not wanting to move, but

I'd already pissed in an empty soda bottle, and I needed food. I was tired as fuck, too.

"Thanks," I replied, knowing I had to leave her.

He nodded and went back to his truck.

I watched him settle into his seat before I pulled away. It was fucking hard, but I knew Boyd would take care of her.

A few hours later, I returned. Rand had taken Boyd's spot. I got out and hopped into his passenger seat. I handed him the to-go cup of coffee meant for Boyd.

"Haven't seen a thing," he said, angling his head toward the house then taking a sip of the hot drink.

I looked the place over and panic settled in. "You sure she's in there? What if we're watching a fucking empty—"

"Brother, she's there. Audrey said she's on administrative leave because of everything going on. Audrey texted with her when I swapped with Boyd. Becky hasn't gotten out of bed."

She hasn't gotten out of bed. While that idea would normally be sexy as fuck, it made my wolf want to howl. I'd hurt her. Bad. This was all my fault. She thought I was a monster.

"She needs to eat," I growled. "I bet that kitchen doesn't have an avocado in it."

He ran his hand over his face, studied the house as if answers were painted on it. "I've got an idea. You got it from here?"

I nodded then climbed from his truck and back to mine.

He drove off. I didn't know what the idea was, but it had better be fucking good.

An hour later, I was ready to peek in the bedroom window to check on her like her deadbeat, dead ex, but Rand pulled up behind me. With Mom.

She hopped out in her heavy boots, thick coat and hat, holding covered dishes. She sported a narrowed gaze I recognized as one that said "get out of my way, I've got shit to accomplish."

Fuck, yes.

Rand was brilliant. Mom had food and hugs and everything Becky needed.

BECKY

I HEARD the doorbell but ignored it. I heard the knock on the door and ignored that too. When my cell rang, I flopped over in bed and reached for it on the nightstand.

Audrey had texted earlier to check on me. I knew she worked today since I'd been supposed to work with her. Administrative leave was a bitch because I had nowhere to go. Nothing to do. No money. I hadn't heard from the sheriff to know if I was still under suspicion of Todd's death.

I knew who'd done it, but it wasn't like I could waltz on in and tell the guy a shifter ripped Todd's throat out because my mate, who'd bitten me with his sharp teeth and claimed me for life, was a wolf enforcer who'd shot the guy's cousin in the head and he wanted revenge.

They'd think I was nuts. And I was.

After the night before? How could I not be? The man I loved was part wolf. Wholly dangerous.

I read the text.

It's Janet. I'm at the door. Let me in. I'm cold, and my hands are full of seven-layer dip and barbequed cocktail wieners.

My stomach growled and had me hopping out of bed at the mention of tiny hot dogs. The last few times I'd thrown up, it hadn't been from morning sickness. It appeared I might have gotten past the nauseated phase—thank God—but hadn't lost my weird hankerings.

I all but tossed open the door, and there was Janet with plastic containers in her hands. I grabbed them from her, and she laughed, breezing in as if it were July and not snowing. "Honey, I didn't know which one sounded good right now, so I made you both. No reason to even get a plate, huh?"

She bustled me toward the small kitchen and settled me at the table. I had no idea if she'd been to Audrey's house before or not, but she went directly to the silverware drawer and pulled out a fork.

I took off a lid as she brought me the utensil and grabbed a napkin from the little holder in the center of the table.

The scent of tangy barbecue sauce and meat wafted from the first container I opened. "Oh my God, these look so good."

As Janet took off her coat, she smiled. "All my boys like them. I'd put them in the slow cooker because the boys loved to snack after school."

"That sounds nice for them."

I'd tried to block visions of Clint, but instantly a ten-year old version popped into my head, all tousle haired and rowdy, ready to chow down for a snack.

"You must've bought a lot of food," I said, shoving

a cocktail wiener in my face. It was still warm, and the sauce was sticky and sweet. I closed my eyes as I chewed. Sooo good.

"I did. When Rob, Colton and Boyd lost their parents, we pretty much took care of them. They stayed at the main house... it's their home and all, but I made sure those guys were fed and sorted. Still do, at least a little bit." She sat quietly as I savored the flavor. I hadn't eaten anything since the night before. "The baby's happy now?"

After I swallowed, I speared another and shoveled it in. "Mmmhmm," I replied.

"You've got a big job going on inside you. If you want little hot dogs, then you can have little hot dogs." She reached for the second container and took off the lid.

Seven-layer dip, about three inches thick, only the top layer of thickly spread guacamole with olive halves sprinkled on top visible.

"God, that looks good, too." My mouth was full, and I was eating like a pig.

She held up a spoon. "It doesn't even need chips, does it?"

I shook my head, grabbed the spoon and dug in, getting every bit of the seven layers piled on.

This went in, the flavors of barbeque, refried

beans and sour cream melding on my tongue. I had no idea something so disgusting could be so good.

"You're a really good cook," I told her after she brought me a glass of water to wash it all down.

"Thank you. It's bribery. My boys want good food. They sit at my table."

"That's devious but smart."

"It got you to open the door, didn't it?"

I pointed the spoon at her before digging up some more dip. "You're a good mom," I said. "Trust me, I know bad ones."

She patted my hand and gave me a small smile. "Want to tell me about yours?"

I sighed, taking a break from stuffing my face. I'd eaten all but two little hot dogs and half the dip. I wiped my mouth with the napkin then looked down and saw a glop of barbeque sauce on my shirt. I tried wiping at it, but Janet stilled my hand. I could only imagine what I looked like. I'd cried myself to sleep, and my hair was a snarl. I was wearing Audrey's hand-me-downs that didn't fit all that well. I put the napkin down. A stain on my shirt wasn't going to make me look worse.

"The short version?"

She nodded. "Sure."

"My parents are... religious. The kind who

preach but mess up on the practice part. They weren't married when my mom got pregnant. There was a quickie marriage, and I was *born early.*"

Janet's dark brows went up, but she said nothing.

"They believe marriage is for life. That what God has joined together, no man shall put asunder and all that. It didn't matter if they didn't like each other. Or blamed their loveless marriage on me. My ex... well, he never did become my ex, did he?" I gave a humorless laugh and took a little drink. "*Todd* wasn't a nice guy." I told her about leaving Todd and how he refused to divorce me. "My parents sided with Todd. I should have been a better wife and all that. Staying and being miserable was what was important to them. I didn't agree, and now we don't talk. Pretty much, it was Todd or me, and they chose Todd."

Janet clucked her tongue and gave me a soft smile. "We favor marriage for life, too. By *we,* I mean shifters. And we don't marry, we mate. But you know all that. Now. The difference is, males would never hurt their mate, either emotionally or physically. *Never.*"

I nodded.

"Males are also as dumb as a box of rocks."

I had a spoonful of dip halfway to my mouth

when she said that. I dropped it back in the container and laughed.

"It's true," she said. She put her hand to her dark hair and patted it. "I have a mate, two boys of my own and the Wolf three. Plus a few other friends they've all brought home over the years. If you have questions about shifters, specifically *male* shifters... even more specifically about male shifters I've birthed, then fire away."

I pushed back my chair and stood. Went to the fridge and opened it. Then shut it. God, did I have questions. Glancing over my shoulder at her, I said, "I... I don't know if I'm ready for the answers."

I opened the freezer, found a tub of Rocky Road ice cream and pulled it out. "Want some?" I asked.

"No, honey. Thank you."

I dropped back into my chair, ripped off the lid. After grabbing the spoon from the dip and licking it clean, I scooped up some ice cream.

"Why didn't he tell me?" I asked.

She sighed. "Box of rocks, remember? Did Audrey tell you how she found out Boyd was a shifter?"

"She didn't tell me Boyd *was* a shifter."

"She couldn't, honey. I know she's your best friend, but pack law is stronger than human friendships. She'd be endangering her mate and her unborn child if she did."

"Toss in the baby and make me feel bad," I grumbled.

"She found out when a teenage shifter got shot, and he shifted while she was helping him."

My eyes widened. "Is he okay?"

She smiled at my concern. "Of course. Shifters have rapid healing abilities. But Boyd didn't tell her before she discovered it the hard way. Marina found out when the barn roof collapsed at Audrey's wedding reception." She patted my hand again. "Audrey didn't tell Marina either."

I gasped. "She didn't? Her own sister? Oh man, she must have been furious."

"My point is, the guys are idiots. They think we females can't handle tough stuff. They love to protect us, even from the things we need to know."

"I didn't even know I was mated." I stared at her then blushed. "Oh my God, you knew."

She nodded and smiled. "I am so happy to know Clint's claimed you."

"It's because I'm having his baby." I poked the ice cream.

"Definitely."

That hurt. A lot. I stared at the lumps of

chocolate in the ice cream. "I don't want Clint if that's all he wants. Todd didn't really want me. He wanted a possession. My parents felt obliged to save face."

"Honey—"

"I won't be an obligation."

"Male shifters aren't like human men. The first time Clint breathed in your scent, he knew you were his. Forever."

"That's insane. His nose was broken the first time we met. That meant that... oh my God, I threw up on him."

She laughed. "Yet he still wanted you."

I covered my face with my hand. "He did."

"The wolf finds his mate by scent. That's how Tom found me. How Boyd knew Audrey was the one. The same went for Colton and Marina. Even Rob, and he's alpha. You're Clint's. Baby or not. That's it. The entire love story from his perspective is right there."

"Seriously?"

She nodded. "You're human, so you don't have the same response right back. It's much easier when it's a shifter-shifter match."

"I bet."

"This is what's probably torturing Clint right

now—that you don't understand the depth of what he feels for you. He's never once questioned you being for him, and he never will."

"You're his mother, you have to say stuff like that."

She shook her head. "I'm a shifter. It's easy because when a son says he's met his mate, he's met his mate. Do you... do you care about him?"

I poked at the ice cream some more. "Yes."

"Do you want him... forever?"

"I thought so, but... Janet, he's... I won't say because you're his mom."

"He's an enforcer. I've heard. As a shifter parent, I couldn't be more proud."

My mouth fell open. "He *kills* people. I saw firsthand last night."

She shook her head. "He kills rogue shifters. He does it under orders. Do you think snipers in the military are bad?"

I frowned. "They're doing their jobs taking out bad guys."

"Exactly."

I blinked. "It was scary."

She offered me a small smile. "I bet. Wolves fight. The customs are different. It's complicated, but you'll grow to understand."

"He left me here alone. If he's so protective, where is he?"

She laughed and pointed toward the front door. "Go look out the window."

I popped up and went to the front window. There was Clint, across the street in his truck.

"He was there all night. Others took his place earlier, so he could rest, but he'll be there all night again."

"But…"

"You're his mate, Becky. He'll never leave you. Never leave you unprotected. You're cherished and loved, watched over, even if you refuse him."

I turned to look at her. "You're kidding."

She shook her head. "He'll watch out for you and the baby no matter what. Knowing he's an enforcer means he's going to be even more diligent."

"That's crazy."

"Remember, I said they're dumbasses?"

I nodded, biting my lip as I stared at Clint. He was looking out the side window at the house, right at me. I had no idea if he could see me or not, but it was as if he could sense me.

"We females need to keep them in line. You're doing a mighty fine job of it with Clint. You've got to make them think they're in charge, but really, you've got them all figured out. You're gonna raise that granddaughter of mine to wrap Clint around her little finger too."

"You're devious."

Clint was dangerous but not to me. He'd fought that… wolf last night because I'd been in danger. He'd risked his life for us, and I had a feeling he'd do it again. He took care of his own, his pack… or me, his mate.

Oh my God. Clint did it all for me. It was a shifter way of showing me his love. A gruesome, bloody, naked way to do it, but still…

"We females have to be," she continued. "The males, they're also loyal and loveable and sweet and—"

I gasped, my hand flying to my belly. The baby had kicked. Or rather, it was the first time I felt my baby kick. Our baby.

"Is it the quickening?" Janet asked.

I nodded, eyes misting. Call me sappy, but it felt like a sign. I may not know a man's my mate by his scent, but the way my body leaned toward that window, toward Clint…

The way it felt so wrong to be apart from him— that had to mean something.

I'd lumped him in with Todd for his dishonesty,

but he was the opposite. He wasn't manipulating me. He didn't make me wrong. He hadn't shown up here last night with demands. When I told him not to call, he'd honored my request. And yet he'd still driven into town and stayed all night long—in freezing weather—watching over me.

With a sob, I flung open the door and ran toward Clint, just like at the police station. He was there, would always be there, waiting for me. Protecting me even when he couldn't himself.

Instantly, he climbed out and stalked toward me, opening his arms when he got close.

I leaped at him, wrapping my arms around his neck, my legs around his waist. A hand cupped my ass to hold me as the other sank into my hair.

"Sugar."

We stood on the front lawn and kissed. And kissed. I wasn't cold. I didn't feel anything but every inch of Clint's hard body and heat.

"My job here is done," Janet said. "Get her inside, Clint. Don't be a dumbass and claim her again in the front yard."

25

Clint

If my mate wasn't in my arms, I would've dropped to my knees, humbled by the grace of fate to bring her willingly back to me.

"Sugar," I croaked, barely hearing my mom. "Please forgive me." I wasn't a guy of many words, but I had a million to say to her right now.

Everything I would've said from the beginning, if I'd been able. Everything she deserved to know. She'd given me everything, and I'd had to keep secrets. No longer.

"Clint." There were tears caught on the one word, and it fucking killed me knowing I'd put them there.

I carried her back into Audrey's house and tossed my jacket on the couch, never putting her down. My wolf wanted me to carry her straight to the bedroom and claim her again. Satisfy her until she screamed my name for all the neighbors to hear. But we needed to talk. I needed to know she forgave me.

I kept her cradled in my arms but sat in an armchair, arranging her on my lap. I couldn't bear to let her out of my embrace, even for our talk. Her scent soothed me, calmed my wolf. She felt soft and warm. I'd recognize every inch of her anywhere.

My hands settled on her hips, my thumbs stroking over the curves of her ass. "Sugar, I'm so sorry. I wish to fuck I could have a do-over with you. I'd do it all different."

Her blue eyes searched my face, vulnerability showing there. I wouldn't tell her this aloud, but she looked a mess. It was like a poisoned blade to the gut knowing I'd made her cry all night. That her hair was matted on one side, that her top had... sauce on it. Yet even with all that, she was the most beautiful thing in the whole world.

"Yeah? What would you do?"

I groaned. "Well, first of all, I'd have figured out you were my mate that night at Cody's. I didn't get your scent, but my body sure as hell responded to you. My wolf, too. Even after I let you get back to your friends, I didn't want it to be a one-night fling. I should've known it was because you were mine."

She touched the place I'd marked her.

"And that," I lifted my chin toward it. "I'm so fucking sorry. I never meant to mark you without your permission. That was so shitty. It was an accident. My wolf was just so fucking satisfied to have you under me, I just…"

"Slipped?" Her lips twisted into a smile.

I let out a relieved laugh at seeing it on her. "Yeah, I slipped. Take it as a compliment. You made me lose complete control. You do, every time we're together."

She snuggled in my lap, wiggling her ass around to get comfortable. Of course, my dick took that as an invitation to get harder than stone. "Your mom told me a little but tell me about this bite. Not the concept of it but *my* actual one. What does it mean?"

I stroked my thumb across her cheek, grateful for having the privilege of touching her again. "Sugar, it means I'm your man. Forever. Remember I told you about wolves mating for life?"

I was close enough to see her pulse quicken. Hear her little intake of breath.

"I remember."

"It's true of shifter wolves, too. We're loyal to the death. To our pack, to our families and *especially—always*—to our mate."

"What if I'd told you I didn't want you to bite me?"

I winced. "That would've been very difficult for me. I would've tried to respect your wishes—of course—but my instinct to claim you was so strong." I grinned. "You might've needed to tie me up before we had sex."

Her breath quickened, and she squirmed in my lap. "Well, that sounds hot."

"Well, it's still on the table, if that's what you're into, sugar." Anything to get my sweet human back in the sheets. Anything to satisfy her. "Remember, if you have needs, it's my job to see to them. Whatever they are."

"What about Todd? I'm still--"

I shook my head. "You're not a suspect. Selena called while I was in the car. You've been cleared. With Donald dead, they'll never discover the truth."

"It's over," she repeated.

"There's his estate to clear up, but Selena said she'd handle it for you."

"I don't want to think of him anymore." She bit her lip. "As for us, if I had it to do over, I would've given you my number that night at Cody's," she said, kindling warmth in my chest. "Or told you when I found out I was pregnant." She ducked her head. "It was... disrespectful, especially knowing now how you feel about family. You, personally, and shifters in general. I'm not used to parents really wanting their kids."

"Sugar," I said with a sigh, my thumb stroking her cheek again.

"You took that revelation a lot more gracefully than I took yours. I'm sorry, too."

I closed my eyes. "I've killed people. You saw it. That will never go away."

She looked at me with sad eyes. "Your mom said your job was like being in the military, being ordered to kill the bad guys. Killing is killing, but you were justified. Last night, you were protecting us."

"Sugar," I said, the one word pained.

"I know the difference between good and bad. You're *good*."

I cradled her face and pulled her head down to kiss her forehead. Was it really that simple? I owed my mom a lot. Thank fuck she could explain shit better than me. "Yesterday was a disaster from start to finish, and it was all my fault. I'm sorry you had to go through it. But I want you to know that I tendered my resignation as council enforcer as soon as I marked you. I didn't want to be away from you. I didn't want the job. What it meant. I will never invite danger near our family again. While I can't say I'll never kill again, I'll only do it to protect what's mine. Our family."

"Our family," she whispered, reaching out to touch her fingertips to my lips. "I like the way that sounds."

"That's what I want, sugar. Desperately. I'll do anything to have you. Please say you'll give me a redo."

She laughed a watery laugh. "I'll totally give you a redo. Does that mean we're going back to Cody's?"

I chuckled. "I wouldn't mind getting you in that storeroom again. Although I don't know if fucking hard up against a wall is the best thing for the baby."

She smirked. "It's fine for the baby, but we'd better do it soon because in a month or two my belly will get too big for that."

"There's lots of ways I can take you. Don't you worry none about that." I slid my palm over her sweet baby bump. "I can't fucking wait for you to get big. You're already the most beautiful pregnant female on the planet."

She pushed my hand lower, between her legs, and I didn't bite back the growl.

Her brows shot up and eyes widened with excitement. "Ooh. I think your wolf wants me."

I launched myself out of the armchair, already carrying her toward the bedroom. "Sugar, my wolf always wants you. We're talking twenty-four-seven." I lowered her onto the bed and pulled her pajama bottoms and panties off. "I'm wild for you."

"Uh uh." She sat up and reached for my shirt, yanking the snaps open to reveal my chest. "Where's the rope?"

26

Clint

Oh, damn. I wasn't going to last five minutes. Maybe not even two. The idea of Becky tying me up and having her way with me had my balls tight, my cock painfully thick.

I shucked my clothes while she searched Audrey's drawers and produced a pair of tights. "These should work," she said.

They would. Certainly not because I couldn't get free of them. Nothing she could tie me up with could actually hold me, but for her, I'd follow any command. I let her wrap my wrists and attach them to one of the bed posts then watched avidly as she stripped off her pajama top and cupped her beautiful breasts.

Holy. Fuck. She was lush and curvy and perfect. Her tits were even bigger, the nipples enlarging too. More to suck and lick and nip.

"You've had your mouth on me, but I haven't had a chance to return the favor." She crawled on the bed in a slow seduction. She had no idea just how hot she was. I clenched my fists trying not to rip the tights to shreds and grab her.

My cock jutted out perpendicular to the bed, bobbing for her attention. Pre-cum dripped down the crown.

"Oh, sugar," I muttered, my chest already heaving. "I'm not gonna last, and that's going to be a problem."

She rubbed her lips together as she approached, and I couldn't take my eyes away from them. "Why is that a problem?"

"Because I need to get you off. Like, fucking soon." I tossed my hips into the air and rolled them.

She laughed, maybe because I sounded as desperate as I felt. When she gripped the base of my cock, some of that pre-cum dribbled down over her hand. I was so fucking ready.

"Becky, I love you." I spoke fast, needing to get

the words out before I lost my mind. Especially when she lowered her head and licked slowly around the head of my purpled member. "It's not just biology," I grit out. "Not just because my wolf picked you or fate picked you. Oh *fuck*." I shuddered as she lowered her mouth over my length and took me all the way into the pocket of her cheek.

My balls drew up, and I felt my orgasm build at the base of my spine. Sweat dotted my brow. I was going to die of pleasure, and when I looked down at her, watched the way my dick disappeared in that mouth of hers...

"Mmm?" she hummed around my dick, and I shoved my hips up, accidentally forcing her to take me deeper. I'd never felt anything better. So hot. Wet. The suction... fuck!

"Oh fates. I-I just want you to know that. I love you for you. Strong, independent. Smart. Capable. Sassy. Beautiful. Oh *gawd*."

"Mmmm," she hummed her agreement, picking up speed as she bobbed over my length.

"Fuck, Becky. Fuck." My thighs flexed. I dug my heels into the mattress, trying not to jack my hips up and ram my cock down her throat. But it felt. So. Good.

"Becky, Becky, Becky, Becky."

She popped off and laughed. "Whose name do you scream when you come?" she demanded, mocking the question I'd made her answer up at the cabin.

I fisted the sheets, wrestling for control. "Yours. Only yours. It will only ever be yours, sugar. Forever."

I smelled the scent of her arousal as she bobbed faster and faster over my dick, hollowing out her cheeks to suck me hard. I loved that this was turning her on, too. I just wanted to be able to get her off. "Ride me," I choked. "Ride me, sugar and let me watch those full tits bounce," I begged. "Let me see that little bump that shows me how I got my cum up and in you and made a pup."

She popped off my dick, licking her lips with a Cheshire cat smile. "You want me to ride you, cowboy?" she drawled, gripping the base tight as she slowly mounted my hips.

My shudder of pleasure was visible and made her smile wider. "Aw, please, sugar. Please. I want to see you get off when I do."

She lifted her hips then impaled herself on my dick.

I shouted with the pleasure of it. So good. So good. Her walls clenched around me. The bedroom was bright, and I could see all of her. There was no shyness now. Hell, there never had been any. It had been secrets that had kept us in the dark, but now… now we could show each other everything.

She braced her hands on my shoulders and started to undulate her hips slowly, rocking over my dick, grinding her sweet little clitty down against the root.

I had to work hard to resist the urge to break free of the tights and grip her hips, move her over my manhood in a way that would make both of us go mad. She wanted to be in charge now, and that was hot in itself. I loved watching how she moved, how she liked it.

She slowly picked up speed, and I watched her tits swing up and down, her nipples hard thick points—thicker than they'd been pre-pregnancy. Fucking gorgeous.

I thrust my hips up to match her rhythm, pushing in deeper, trying to bring friction to her clit and hit her g-spot.

"Beautiful, beautiful human," I murmured.

She got wetter. "Devilish wolf."

I squeezed my eyes closed because my need was getting too strong. She sped up, gliding over me, forward and back. I popped my eyes back open.

"Show me how you come, sugar. Show me how you ride daddy's dick until you come."

"Daddy's dick?" she laughed, panting. "Now that's some kinky shit."

"Uh huh. And you love every minute of it." I knew because she'd gushed fresh arousal down my cock when I said it.

"Oh God," she moaned. Her face was flushed. She reached up and untied the tights. "You'd better help me. I'm getting dizzy. Fifty percent more blood volume and all that."

I gripped her hips and took over the effort, moving her forward and back so she could just go along for the ride. "You want to stay on top, or do you need daddy to flip you on your back and fuck you hard?"

Her pussy clenched around my dick with the dirty talk. She was already coming. "Flip me, daddy." She grinned then groaned.

In one smooth motion, I swapped our positions, carefully laying her on her back, so I could get even deeper inside her.

She threw her arms up by her head in surrender, her eyes already rolling back, lashes fluttering. Her back arched, and her tits thrust up toward my mouth. "Oh God…"

"That's it, sugar." I fucked her hard and fast, already past my own breaking point. The bed slammed against the wall, cracking the plaster. Oops. *Sorry, Audrey!*

She lifted her legs in the air in a wide spread eagle allowing me to pump even harder. Deeper. Faster. I grabbed a knee, held on.

"Becky," I croaked.

She screamed and reached for my shoulders, her nails digging in. She locked her ankles behind my back and yanked my hips in to stay as her sweet, tight channel gripped my dick in quick pulses. I'd have thought she was even more responsive, more sensitive because of being pregnant, but this was all Becky. Us. We were wild and frenzied together. Always.

I continued to pump, taking her hips with mine as I reached the peak and hurtled over the other side.

"Oh *fuck!*" I shouted. "Becky, Becky, Becky, Becky." My release had to be one for the record books. I seriously don't see how I could've come any harder or more. Heat sizzled across my skin.

"Daddy, Daddy, Daddy, Clint!" she chanted back, laughing through the whole thing, her sweet pussy continuing to milk my dick for its cum.

I went blind for a minute. Maybe longer. The

room sparked with fireworks. I couldn't breathe, but that wasn't important because all that mattered was how good she felt.

And then I found myself covering Becky's body with my own, nuzzling into her neck and whispering nonsense to her, careful of the slight curve.

"Marry me?" I asked because she was human, and that was their custom. Willow and Rob hadn't had a wedding, but Marina and Audrey had both had weddings to mark the human version of a mating.

She didn't answer, so I pulled back to look at her face, my heart jumping up to choke my throat. Fuck. Was she still not sure about me? About us?

"Do shifters marry?" she asked. Her cheeks were flushed and her hair damp. She looked well and truly fucked, but a little frown marred her forehead.

I blinked, surprised she'd already picked up enough about our kind to ask the question. I wasn't sure what she and Mom talked about, but I didn't really care. Whatever they'd shared had made all the difference. "No, not usually. Well, we do it on paper at the courthouse to satisfy human laws, but it's not celebrated. The mating is what really matters."

I ran my thumb over the spot on her neck that indicated we were mated for life.

"Then, that's all the matters to me, too." She shook her head. "I've been married. I didn't care for it. If it's just the same to you, I don't want it again. I'd rather try it your way."

I smiled, warmth bleeding back into my body. "Then you're already mine. I can't undo what I've done, and I wouldn't. Rebecca Nichols, will you accept my mating bite?" I asked in the formal tones of a wedding officiant.

She smiled, love and warmth radiating from her beautiful blue gaze. "I've never been so happy *not* getting married. Clint Tucker, I will."

EPILOGUE

*B*ECKY

"It's fine. I'm doing fine," I reassured my mate, whose head looked like it was about to spin around and pop off after my last contraction. "But a little less pressure on the hand."

"Fuck!" Clint released his overly-tight grip, and I shook my fingers out. "Are you sure you don't want an epidural? Sugar, you don't need to be a hero. It's killing me to see you in pain."

"It's not about you, Clint," Janet informed her son tartly, feeding me a spoonful of crushed ice with apple juice mixed in. "You're doing great, honey. And of course, Clint's right--"

"No," I gasped then stopped to breathe through another contraction. They were coming one right on top of the other now, which meant I was definitely in transition. "Don't offer again," I got out when it ebbed.

Clint smacked his head. "I'm sorry. You told me that."

I tried to sit up. "Help me up. I want to walk around."

Clint sent a shocked look at Theresa, the labor and delivery nurse on duty. "Is that allowed?"

"Clint," I growled. I remembered Janet's talk months ago about how the males needed to think they were in charge, watching out and protecting. Well, I was in fucking charge now.

He scooped me up from the hospital bed into his arms, like his idea of me walking around was him carrying me through the halls of the hospital.

True to his word, he'd carried me around until the day I went into labor. I'd arrived in this hospital in his arms, which was definitely going to become a story I'd never live down with my colleagues.

"Put me down. I need gravity to do its work now," I said.

He grumbled as he slowly tipped me to my feet as if I were made of glass. I turned to face him and lifted my arms to his shoulders. I couldn't remember the last time he'd hugged me, my belly so big it was impossible.

"Slow dance?" I asked with a wry smile. He lurched to tuck his arms under mine and hold me up, and I rested my head against his chest, swaying slowly and imagining the head of our sweet baby girl melting my cervix open with each slow figure eight of my hips.

Clint's hold was gentle, almost reverent. He'd been attentive and protective every day. I was thankful for being a labor and delivery nurse, and I knew what to expect; otherwise, he'd have panicked... okay, panicked less and run roughshod over the entire floor. My big guardian with a tender heart.

Time disappeared. I cocooned myself in the love of my mate and everyone else around me-—his family—mine now, our friends, my co-workers. I'd wanted a real family my whole life, and I'd found my partner in Clint. Our family would grow by one soon. She would be loved completely, unconditionally. She already was.

"It's time," I murmured to Theresa, who had

accepted my refusal to have my dilation checked since I entered transition. "Get Audrey."

While Dr. Seymour had seen me all through my pregnancy, she was out of town for spring break with her family. Audrey was working although she'd only been back from her own maternity leave a few weeks. Boyd had insisted she cut her workload in half, and she didn't mind, content to stay home with their baby as much as possible. We'd both laughed about it when I first arrived on the floor, my contractions ten minutes apart, but in the end, I was glad it would be her to help me bring my daughter into the world.

"*What?*" Clint yelped. "How do you know that?" He glanced down as if he could see through the hospital gown a head popping out of my crotch.

"Shh." I tightened my grip on him. My last contraction had become a push. "Put me down on my side and catch your baby."

"*What?*" I have to hand it to Clint. He may have been freaked out, but his movements were quick, strong and sure. He gently lifted me into his arms and laid me carefully on my side in the bed. Janet watched, but she stood out of the way, silent, letting this moment be ours.

I wanted to speak, to tell him to get ready because

she was coming, but forming words became an impossibility. My body was doing what it had been made to do. There was no practice for such a thing. No way to prepare. As much as we humans wanted to control, in the end, our biology knew better—same as shifters finding their mates. Clint had been so sure I was the one for him, that we would be together forever. I was sure about this, about our growing family. My body took over and pushed out our sweet baby.

Clint gulped back a sob. "Her head is out!"

With the next push the rest of her emerged, and Clint caught her in his large hands just as Audrey and Theresa rushed in the room.

"She's here." My big strong mate was weeping. "You did it, sugar. Our baby is here."

"Oh wow, she's here!" Audrey entered swiftly but didn't take over. She stood at Clint's shoulder and let us have our moment.

I met her gaze over Clint's arm. "Is she okay? Is everything all right?"

Audrey gently put a stethoscope to our baby's heart. "She sounds perfect, Becky. Congratulations, mama."

Theresa slipped in to wipe the blood off her and slip a cap on her head before easing her from Clint's ginger grip and placing her in my arms. Clint shifted to my side, sitting on the bed and wrapping a strong arm around my shoulders as I stared down at our miracle.

I didn't have the urge to cry. Maybe I was too stunned. Maybe my body was in shock. Not until I put my baby's mouth to my breast and she latched right on and started sucking did I burst into tears.

"She's so smart," I wept, looking up through my tears at Janet. "Look at her."

Janet also burst into tears. "Yes, look at her. Strong and smart like her mama."

Even Audrey blinked back tears as she helped deliver the afterbirth, cut the cord and stitched me up. Of course, she still had raging hormones going, too, having given birth to her daughter seven weeks ago.

"Happy birthday, Lily," I said, naming her after my favorite flower. I turned questioning eyes on Clint because the name hadn't even been on our shortlist. I hadn't even thought of it before I looked at her beautiful little face.

Clint kissed my temple. "Lily. I love it. Sweet Lily. Happy birthday, precious flower."

I watched, mesmerized by her suckling. "Look at

her tiny lips," I breathed, starting to tremble from the shock.

Clint tightened his arm around my shoulders. "Look at her tiny fingers."

"She's perfect," Janet breathed.

Our sweet baby had drifted to sleep at my breast, drunk on colostrum.

"Let us just check her over and get her cleaned up, okay?" Audrey said.

I nodded and handed over my baby, trusting her completely.

I let my head fall against Clint's shoulder. "We did it."

"*You* did it," he corrected. "You were such a champion. How do you feel?"

"Tired," I murmured. "But also wide awake."

"Food might help," Janet suggested.

I smiled because food was Janet's solution to everything, and I absolutely adored her for it. It was a wonderful way to show love, as far as I was concerned.

After a lifetime of feeling like it was me against the world, I now felt nothing but loved. I was surrounded by so much tenderness—an entire pack of love. My big strong wolf-man who was utterly devoted to me.

And now Lily, this tiny being who had already captured all of our hearts.

Ready for more Wolf Ranch?
Get Fierce next!

Pack Rule #5: Happy mate, happy fate.

Fate has it in for me. She's sent me the sassiest, strong-willed female imaginable. Wolf Ranch's new veterinarian. A human who thinks I do everything wrong. Thinks she knows large animals better than I do. And who doesn't want anything to do with me.

But I knew the first time I caught her scent she belonged to me. So I'll show her a large animal. One she can't resist. Or at least one who can't resist her. I'll prove she doesn't know everything about four-legged beasts. Especially not the fiercest ones who stalk their prey in the night. Especially not one determined to prey on her.

Me.

Read Fierce!

NOTE FROM VANESSA & RENEE

Guess what? We've got some bonus content for you with Clint and Becky. Yup, there's more!

Click here to read!

GET A FREE VANESSA VALE BOOK!

Join my mailing list to be the first to know of new releases, free books, special prices and other author giveaways.

http://freeromanceread.com

WANT FREE RENEE ROSE BOOKS?

Go to http://subscribepage.com/alphastemp to sign up for Renee Rose's newsletter and receive a free copy of *Alpha's Temptation, Theirs to Protect, Owned by the Marine, Theirs to Punish, The Alpha's Punishment, Disobedience at the Dressmaker's* and *Her Billionaire Boss*. In addition to the free stories, you will also get bonus epilogues, special pricing, exclusive previews and news of new releases.

ALSO BY VANESSA VALE

For the most up-to-date listing of my books:

vanessavalebooks.com

On A Manhunt

Man Hunt

Man Candy

Man Cave

The Billion Heirs

Scarred

Flawed

Broken

Alpha Mountain

Hero

Rebel

Warrior

Billionaire Ranch

North

South

East

West

Bachelor Auction

Teach Me The Ropes

Hand Me The Reins

Back In The Saddle

Wolf Ranch

Rough

Wild

Feral

Savage

Fierce

Ruthless

Two Marks

Untamed

Tempted

Desired

Enticed

More Than A Cowboy

Strong & Steady

Rough & Ready

Wild Mountain Men

Mountain Darkness

Mountain Delights

Mountain Desire

Mountain Danger

Grade-A Beefcakes

Sir Loin of Beef

T-Bone

Tri-Tip

Porterhouse

Skirt Steak

Small Town Romance

Montana Fire

Montana Ice

Montana Heat

Montana Wild

Montana Mine

Steele Ranch

Spurred

Wrangled

Tangled

Hitched

Lassoed

Bridgewater County

Ride Me Dirty

Claim Me Hard

Take Me Fast

Hold Me Close

Make Me Yours

Kiss Me Crazy

Mail Order Bride of Slate Springs

A Wanton Woman

A Wild Woman

A Wicked Woman

Bridgewater Ménage

Their Runaway Bride

Their Kidnapped Bride

Their Wayward Bride

Their Captivated Bride

Their Treasured Bride

Their Christmas Bride

Their Reluctant Bride

Their Stolen Bride

Their Brazen Bride

Their Rebellious Bride

Their Reckless Bride

Bridgewater Brides World

Lenox Ranch Cowboys

Cowboys & Kisses

Spurs & Satin

Reins & Ribbons

Brands & Bows

Lassos & Lace

Montana Men

The Lawman

The Cowboy

The Outlaw

Standalones

Relentless

All Mine & Mine To Take

Bride Pact

Rough Love

Twice As Delicious

Flirting With The Law

Mistletoe Marriage

Man Candy - A Coloring Book

OTHER TITLES BY RENEE ROSE

Made Men Series

Don't Tease Me

Don't Tempt Me

Don't Make Me

Chicago Bratva

"Prelude" in Black Light: Roulette War

The Director

The Fixer

"Owned" in Black Light: Roulette Rematch

The Enforcer

The Soldier

The Hacker

The Bookie

The Cleaner

The Player

The Gatekeeper

Alpha Mountain

Hero

Rebel

Warrior

Vegas Underground Mafia Romance

King of Diamonds

Mafia Daddy

Jack of Spades

Ace of Hearts

Joker's Wild

His Queen of Clubs

Dead Man's Hand

Wild Card

Contemporary

Daddy Rules Series

Fire Daddy

Hollywood Daddy

Stepbrother Daddy

Master Me Series

Her Royal Master

Her Russian Master

Her Marine Master

Yes, Doctor

Double Doms Series

Theirs to Punish

Theirs to Protect

Holiday Feel-Good

Scoring with Santa

Saved

Other Contemporary

Black Light: Valentine Roulette

Black Light: Roulette Redux

Black Light: Celebrity Roulette

Black Light: Roulette War

Black Light: Roulette Rematch

Punishing Portia (written as Darling Adams)

The Professor's Girl

Safe in his Arms

Paranormal
Two Marks Series

Untamed

Tempted

Desired

Enticed

Wolf Ranch Series

Rough

Wild

Feral

Savage

Fierce

Ruthless

Wolf Ridge High Series

Alpha Bully

Alpha Knight

Bad Boy Alphas Series

Alpha's Temptation

Alpha's Danger

Alpha's Prize

Alpha's Challenge

Alpha's Obsession

Alpha's Desire

Alpha's War

Alpha's Mission

Alpha's Bane

Alpha's Secret

Alpha's Prey

Alpha's Sun

Shifter Ops

Alpha's Moon

Alpha's Vow

Alpha's Revenge

Alpha's Fire

Alpha's Rescue

Alpha's Command

Midnight Doms

Alpha's Blood

His Captive Mortal

All Souls Night

Alpha Doms Series

The Alpha's Hunger

The Alpha's Promise

The Alpha's Punishment

The Alpha's Protection (Dirty Daddies)

Other Paranormal

The Winter Storm: An Ever After Chronicle

Sci-Fi

Zandian Masters Series

His Human Slave

His Human Prisoner

Training His Human

His Human Rebel

His Human Vessel

His Mate and Master

Zandian Pet

Their Zandian Mate

His Human Possession

Zandian Brides

Night of the Zandians

Bought by the Zandians

Mastered by the Zandians

Zandian Lights

Kept by the Zandian

Claimed by the Zandian

Stolen by the Zandian

Other Sci-Fi

The Hand of Vengeance

Her Alien Masters

ABOUT VANESSA VALE

A USA Today bestseller, Vanessa Vale writes tempting romance with unapologetic bad boys who don't just fall in love, they fall hard. Her books have sold over one million copies. She lives in the American West where she's always finding inspiration for her next story. While she's not as skilled at social media as her kids, she loves to interact with readers.

vanessavaleauthor.com

- facebook.com/vanessavaleauthor
- instagram.com/vanessa_vale_author
- amazon.com/Vanessa-Vale/e/B00PGB3AXC
- bookbub.com/profile/vanessa-vale
- tiktok.com/@vanessavaleauthor

ABOUT RENEE ROSE

USA TODAY BESTSELLING AUTHOR RENEE ROSE loves a dominant, dirty-talking alpha hero! She's sold over two million copies of steamy romance with varying levels of kink. Her books have been featured in USA Today's *Happily Ever After* and *Popsugar*. Named Eroticon USA's Next Top Erotic Author in 2013, she has also won *Spunky and Sassy's* Favorite Sci-Fi and Anthology author, *The Romance Reviews* Best Historical Romance, and *has* hit the *USA Today* list over a dozen times with her Chicago Bratva, Bad Boy Alpha and Wolf Ranch series, as well as various anthologies.

Renee loves to connect with readers!
www.reneeroseromance.com
renee@reneeroseromance.com

- facebook.com/reneeroseromance
- twitter.com/reneeroseauthor
- instagram.com/reneeroseromance
- amazon.com/Renee-Rose/e/B008AS0FT0
- bookbub.com/authors/renee-rose
- tiktok.com/@authorreneerose

Printed in Great Britain
by Amazon